Fleeing from his past, fifteen year-old Brody Martin runs right into trouble. A dead man in the woods, a terrifying creature on his trail, and the Miller clan out for blood has Brody running right into...

The Devil's Trap

"When I shoot, it's going to be right on top of us. You need to run," Brody whispered. The boy stopped crying, but didn't move. "Are you listening, Todd? *You've got to run.*"

The
—— Devil's Trap ——

JAMES BABB

Dedicated in memory of

Coleman Pearson

Read Coleman's Story & about EEE on the last page of this book.

ISBN 978-0-9914921-2-1

$200 REWARD

WE WILL PAY TWO HUNDRED DOLLARS TO BRING IN

Brody Martin

WANTED FOR SUSPICION OF MURDER AND HORSE STEALING

BRODY MARTIN IS SUSPECTED OF HAVING A PART IN THE MURDER OF GORDON "DOC" MILLER SOMETIME IN NOVEMBER, 1880. AND HE IS WANTED FOR STEALING ONE BLACK MARE AND ONE BAY HORSE FROM BILLY MILLER ON THE NIGHT OF DECEMBER 10, 1880.

DESCRIPTION.

Brody Martin is near 5 feet 4 inches tall, 120-130 lbs. weight, thin body, around fifteen years of age, brown eyes, straight brown hair, medium complexion, good even teeth. He has a large scar above his left eye through his eyebrow, has the appearance of being a burn. He is from Sebastian County, and may be hiding in Indian Territory.

He was traveling with a murderer, the negro known only as Amos. Amos is about 45 years of age, tall and lean, curly black hair peppered with gray, has a slight limp and multiple scars. He has deep grooves in his face and has a mean temper.

Send information at my expense to
BILLY MILLER of Sebastian County, Fort Smith, Arkansas

Chapter One

Indian Territory, Spring 1881

B rody eased forward, placing each step carefully. The leaves were damp from the early morning dew, but the twigs underneath were still brittle and crunched under his weight. A large shadow moved deep in the forest and Brody froze.

He kept his eyes focused on the distant shape as it slowly disappeared behind a large tree. He started forward, but hesitated when he heard dead limbs cracking and leaves swishing. Realizing who was coming, Brody paused, shook his head in agitation, and then turned.

He struggled to keep his voice to a whisper. "Todd. I told you to stay with your pa."

The boy's smile faded to a frown but he stood his ground. "But Flint, Father said he was going on down the trail to check the last traps."

Brody sighed heavily. Todd grinned at that, and Brody couldn't help but let go of his aggravation and grin back. He leaned closer to Todd and whispered. "Well, stay close and be quiet. I saw something moving around down there." He pointed to the large oak near the bottom of the ridge and then held his finger against his lips. "I think it's a deer."

Todd nodded. His shaggy black hair shifted back and forth.

Brody turned and carefully picked his way down the wooded hill. Behind him twigs snapped and a soft sound filled the air. *Phawp, phawp, phawp.*

He glared back at Todd. "Stop that."

Todd nodded, made one last popping sound with his mouth, and then cinched his lips tight.

Brody sighed again. He thought Indians were supposed to be sneaky and quiet but Todd was louder than a herd of blind cows coming through a cane patch. "Step where I step, and don't make a sound." He watched Todd using trees to help keep his balance as he struggled to place his feet in Brody's footprints.

They continued down the ridge.

The boy had turned out to be a little younger than Brody first thought. When Todd's father, Joseph Wolf, had offered him a trapping job three months ago at the stables in Fort Smith, Brody had guessed the boy's age at nine or ten but he was wrong. Todd had just turned eight, and had Brody known what a passel of trouble the kid could get into he might have thought twice about signing on with them.

Joseph had been good to Brody, though, and shown great patience while he taught him about trapping. Brody tried to keep that in mind each time Todd made him want to pull his hair out.

They were good people, making Brody feel guilty for lying about his name. He had told Joseph he was called Flint, and immediately regretted it, but he just couldn't risk using his real name. Too many people were looking for him, but when Christmas and the turning of the year came and went quietly, Brody's worries of being a wanted man began to weigh a little less on his mind.

A whistling snort came from ahead. Searching the woods carefully, he spotted the startled deer as it stamped its foot. Brody went to one knee and settled the Henry rifle against his shoulder. He took aim while trying to keep the cracked stock from wobbling about. The gun roared, and Brody thought he glimpsed the deer racing up and over the opposite ridge.

Todd jumped into the air and threw his hands up. "I think you got him!" The boy took off in a dead run the direction the deer had gone.

Brody went after him. "Come back here!"

Todd covered ground quickly. He jumped a fallen tree and ran up the ridge. "I saw him go this way," he hollered.

"Stop, Todd," Brody ordered.

The boy didn't listen and quickly disappeared into the tree line at the top.

Brody strode over the dead tree and hurried after the boy. When he paused, he couldn't hear Todd running anymore. "Where are you?"

While there was no sign of a blood trail, Todd's track was plain as day on a faint game path. He called for Todd again. The boy didn't answer, so Brody quickened his step down into the hollow.

At the edge of a small creek, he spotted Todd. He was standing still, staring at something in the thicket on the other side of the water. Brody walked up behind him. "You know better than to be running through the woods like that. If you broke a leg or stepped in a trap, your father would kill me." Todd hadn't moved. "What are you looking at?"

Todd reached up and tugged on Brody's sleeve. "The deer you shot is right there."

Brody shook his head. "The deer's long gone. I missed him." As he spoke, Brody squatted down by Todd to get a better view through the branches. A black tail flicked through the air but it was no deer. Long coarse hairs flipped upward and then settled back in place.

"Huh. That's a horse."

"A horse!" Todd took off and Brody reached for him, but was a smidge too slow. He splashed across the shallow creek with Brody in hot pursuit.

"Dadgummit, Todd. You don't know who you might be walking up on."

At that moment, the horse came into clear view. Todd and Brody stopped.

Brody could see the animal had been tied to a tree with a thick lead rope. Hipbones pushed against its hide, as did the ribs. The neck was covered in dried blood from two long slashes, from the shoulder almost up to the ears. Flies swarmed the poor horse, making his hide quiver constantly as it tried to shake them off.

It saw them coming and was standing with its head up and ears forward. Suddenly, it sent out a loud and long neigh.

Brody walked past Todd. "Stay here." He reached for the heavy lead rope attached to the halter. The animal spooked and pulled free. It shied back a few steps until the slack in the rope ran out, stopping the horse with a jolt.

"Whoa, boy, easy," Brody murmured to the startled horse. He angled slowly towards its shoulder, careful not to look directly at it. After a moment, hot air blew on Brody's arm, followed by a head butt to his shoulder. The horse nickered. "Good boy." He continued to speak softly to the animal, and slowly took the lead rope in his hand. The horse was a gelding, with a tan hide and black points, and would probably be a fine mount if he were fed up well.

Something poked Brody in the back. "Is he hurt bad, Flint?"

Brody nearly jumped out of his skin. "Todd!"

"Well, is he?"

The buckskin horse gave a pitiful neigh and bumped his head into Brody's chest. Brody smiled and patted him on the nose.

"Seems like he is still pretty lively." Brody waved the flies away. The twin gashes on the gelding's neck were long but fairly shallow. The dried blood had scabbed over the wounds and there didn't seem to be any infection in them.

For all Todd's impulsiveness, he had a way with animals. The horse was already snuffling his clothes, and the little Indian boy gently rubbed the long brown face and grinned from ear to ear.

Brody turned his attention to the area around them. What little undergrowth the horse hadn't eaten was broken and dead, with a large circle trampled down to the bare soil. "He's tore the ground all up trying to get to the water."

"He needs water bad." Todd was already working at the knot holding the lead to the tree. "Can I take him over to the creek for a drink?"

"Yes." Brody helped Todd get the buckskin untied. "When an animal has been away from water for several days, his stomach shrinks up. Let him drink a few mouthfuls, then pull him away for a little bit before you let him have more. We don't want him sick."

The horse nosed them, as if to tell them to hurry, and Brody patted the animal's side. His coat was rough, and as it slipped through his fingers, wads of shed hair stuck to him. He finished untying the knot and handed the rope to Todd.

"Wrap this line once around that dead tree when you get to the creek. It will help you pull the gelding back from the water."

Todd nodded, more serious than Brody had ever seen him.

Upon discovering it was no longer tied, the horse drug Todd across the ground. Todd gripped the lead with both hands and his feet slid until the buckskin reached the stream. The boy scrambled back to the dead tree and followed Brody's instructions. A comical tug of war followed between the obviously still thirsty horse and a stubborn Indian boy determined to keep his new friend from getting sick.

"Hey, Flint?" Todd asked breathlessly, "Can we take him with us?"

"He's not ours to take. Someone left him tied to that tree."

"Well, they must not want him, or they would take better care of him."

Brody privately agreed with that. "Remember, don't let him drink too much and don't leave him. I'll be back in a minute."

Brody began to circle the area, watching for any signs that might explain why a horse had been left in the middle of the woods, tied to a tree.

Near the creek, but farther upstream, he was surprised to see a brown coat on the creek bank's edge. Brush hid part of it from his sight, so he wasn't sure if it was just a cast-off, or if someone could be in it.

Wary, he watched a minute for any movement. The woods surrounding him seem to close in a bit more, and he couldn't help but check over his shoulder. When he looked back at the coat, it was still in the same position.

A few steps closer, a hand came into view. His feet stopped of their own accord, and his blood ran cold. One of the man's arms was next to the creek, his fingers almost in the water. He was on his stomach with his head turned away.

Brody forced his legs to move closer to the man. The exposed skin was pale. The back of the coat had two long rips side by side, each coated with dried blood and flies. Just like the neck of the horse.

He had only seen a dead man once before. Doc Miller was charging forward with his horse and buggy, about to trample Brody's friend, an ex-slave called Ames. Brody shot the horse to save him, but the wagon flipped over, crushing Doc Miller underneath. It still made Brody sick to remember the feel of the dead man's hand as he pulled him from beneath the broken mess.

He stared down at the body. There was no way he could touch him. A dark wool blanket lay on the ground nearby, as if the man had dropped it before he fell. Brody snatched it up and flung it across the man, then turned and fled through the woods. He had to get Todd, then get to Joseph as quickly as possible.

The boy was rubbing the horse all over with wadded up pine needles, and hair floated in the air all around them. The horse nickered when it saw Brody and chewed on a clump of weeds hanging out of its mouth.

Grabbing Todd by the arm, Brody started back the way they had come earlier, boy and horse in tow.

Todd tried to pull away. "Where we going?"

"To find your daddy."

A loud *thud* of a falling branch as it hit the forest floor came over the top of the ridge. Brody stopped and hushed Todd's protests. Something heavy was walking in the leaves and coming down toward them. Kneeling, Brody placed the wobbly Henry stock against his shoulder. A suddenly silent Todd eased behind him and waited. The sound of crunching leaves grew louder.

Through the thick trees, Brody caught a glimpse of a familiar sight. "It's your father," he said over his shoulder to Todd.

As Joseph came out of the wood line, Brody stood up and waved the Henry in the air.

The big man was a welcome sight. Tall and broad-shouldered, Joseph was a full-blood Cherokee, who knew more about the habits of wild animals and their ways than anybody Brody had ever met.

The bone and turquoise necklace he always wore flopped out of his buckskin jacket. Joseph reached up and absently tucked it back inside. "Where did you find that skinny thing?"

Todd ran over, grabbed his father's hand, and pulled him toward the horse. "He's been left here all alone, and he's hurt, and I let him drink, but not too much so he wouldn't get sick, and we need to take him back with us!"

"Joe," Brody said quietly, "I really need to show you something."

Joseph stared at Brody, then nodded. He wrapped his calloused hand around Todd's wrist. "Son, keep a close eye on this poor old horse. I will be right back."

Todd released his father's hand and gathered up another handful of pine needles. "I'm gonna brush him some more."

Brody waited until Todd was fully occupied with the buckskin, then motioned for Joseph to follow him. "Come and look at this."

As they reached the body, Brody's stomach tightened up and he turned to Joseph. The trapper's face lost all expression. Brody watched him turn a slow, full circle, sure that Joseph was seeing more than just woods and creek and brush. Finally, the large man knelt down by the body and studied it before reaching to take off the blanket.

Brody leaned over. "What do you think happened to him?"

Joseph shook his head, and moved one of the man's arms. A pain filled moan filled the air. Brody scrambled back in shock. "He's alive?"

There was another faint groan.

"Flint, get back over here." Joseph crouched down near the man's face.

Brody came closer, kneeling next to Joseph. He could see only one of the wounded man's eyes. The other was hidden in the sandy dirt. The man's brown hair was streaked in dried mud. Pain contorted his gaunt face and his mouth opened. A guttural moan that almost sounded like words came out.

Brody looked helplessly at Joseph, "Is he speaking English?"

Joseph shook his head and pushed back up to his knees. He glanced down at the man's legs. "He is wearing his long underwear." He placed his hand on the man's shoulder. "What happened to you?"

A mournful sound slowly formed into words. "Hunhh… it's out … thuh… there."

Brody leaned closer to him. "What's out there?"

"Ahhhn… d-d-devil." The man coughed and grimaced in pain. "Verrr… vulf…."

"What?" That didn't make sense, so Brody asked, "What's your name?"

The man closed his eye and became still.

Joseph shook him gently, "What is your name?"

He shivered violently and coughed again. "St-..Stevuhn… Stout. Fort… Fort Smith. Buh-… bury me wit… my vife."
A long breath passed slowly through his lips and he did not take another.

Brody watched the sand under the man's nose. No more breaths disturbed the tiny grains.

Joseph spread the blanket on the ground, next to the body. "He is gone."

Brody said a silent prayer of peace for the man's soul.

He had no desire to touch the man, but under Joseph's stern gaze, he helped roll him over and onto the blanket. The coat opened and revealed two deep slashes across the man's chest. Blood soaked the torn cloth.

After wrapping the body with the blanket, Joseph stood. "Some animal got him. A bear, maybe, or big cat."

"Are you sure?" Brody asked.

Joseph didn't answer. Brody may only have spent one trapping season with the usually chatty Cherokee, but he knew Joseph wasn't sure at all.

Joseph pointed at the creek. "See those stones in the shallows? Tell me what you see."

Brody knew Joseph was testing his tracking skills. He took his time, and then it came to him. "Some of the stones have slide marks where he walked on them. He came up the creek."

"Was the horse tied up?"

Brody nodded.

"Did you find a saddle or any other tack nearby?"

"No sir."

Looking up and down the creek, Joseph said, "He wanted whatever was after him to get the horse and not find his trail. He was running scared." Joseph started back toward Todd and the horse. "He may have been a squatter. They are always trespassing."

Brody followed, glancing back at the body.

Joseph noticed. "Do not worry. We will take him to Fort Smith to be buried."

Brody nodded, but that wasn't exactly what worried him. Something killed that man, and that something was still out there.

Chapter Two

Todd grabbed his father's hand and pulled him. "Come look. Something scratched Buck."

"You should not name him," Joseph said. "He is not ours."

"But he's all alone," Todd argued.

Reaching over and squeezing Brody's shoulder, Joseph said, "Flint will take you back to camp. I will bring the horse along shortly."

Todd clutched the horse's lead rope. "But I want to stay with Buck."

Joseph stared at Todd. "Go."

The boy wilted and started toward the creek.

Joseph leaned toward Brody. "I will get the body on the horse and back to camp." He paused and watched his son splash across the creek with overly heavy steps. He turned back to Brody and met his eyes. "Keep a close watch on Todd."

Brody nodded. Holding the rifle tight, he crossed the stream and caught up to Todd. He watched the woods, looking for the slightest movement. Visions of bears and even worse creatures of the imagination haunted him.

The pine knot oozed sap that sizzled in the flames and flared up. Brody placed several small limbs against the chunk of wood, then got up to find bigger ones to feed the growing fire.

Bam! The heavy camp-shed door slammed behind Todd as he ran out waving a stick with a fox tail tied to the end. He shook the tail in Brody's face, swiping it across his nose. "Tickle, tickle."

"Stop that." Brody grabbed at the stick but Todd ran off, giggling as he went.

"Stay close to camp," Brody warned for the hundredth time that evening.

"Come play with me." Todd circled around and dashed past him again.

"Sit down here and stop running around." Brody saw movement in the tree line. He stood and grabbed his gun.

Joseph rode out of the woods on his bay mare, leading the buckskin behind him with the dead man tied across its back. Joseph's other horse, a brown and white paint, was tied to a rope between two trees. The picket line was near the wagon. The horse started nickering at the new arrival and within seconds, all three horses were neighing at each other.

Todd dropped the fox tail and ran to Joseph's side. "Can I pet Buck?"

Joseph got down and led the horses into camp. "His name is not Buck, little cub."

"What's his name, then?"

"I do not know."

"I want him to be Buck."

Joseph handed the lead rope to Brody, and the poor horse strained its neck, trying to reach the sprigs of grass at the edge of the clearing. "Todd, fetch a bag of feed for our new friend."

Todd started away but stopped. "What's in the blanket?"

Looking at Brody and then to Todd, Joseph said, "A body. Go get the grain."

Todd's brown eyes grew large. "A dead someone?"

Joseph tied the horse's lead to a tree. "Yes. A dead man. Get the feed."

Todd went back over, reached up, and poked at the blanket. "Did you kill him?"

"No."

"Who killed him?"

Removing his hat, Joseph acted as if he was going to swat him with it. "Go on and stop asking questions."

Todd squealed and ran for the wagon. He shouted back, "Is that Buck's owner?"

Brody got a currycomb and started brushing the buckskin. Joseph lowered his big frame down on the log by the fire. A bead of sweat ran down his long hooknose. He wiped his face with his sleeve.

Todd came back with a feedbag. "Did Buck belong to him? Where was he? Who killed him, Flint?"

Brody glanced at Joseph. "We don't know."

Todd turned around to face the buckskin again. "Can I look?"

"No," Joseph said. "Get that feed bag on the horse before he eats through his lead, and then go inside and fetch some beans and salted pork."

"I'm not hungry," Todd whined. Brody hid a smile and took the feedbag from the boy.

"Boy." Joseph growled.

"Yes, sir," he said, picking up his fox tail and disappearing inside the shack.

Brody looked up to see Joseph motion to him. He patted Buck and hung the currycomb on a branch, before settling on a stump next to the trapper.

"We have to take him," Joseph said.

"Where?"

"To Fort Smith to be buried as he asked."

Brody tossed a stick into the fire. "What was he doing out here? Trapping?"

Joseph stood. "Probably not. More likely looking for a place to squat on."

"A trespasser?" Brody asked.

"I would have to guess so. All of the land around these mountains is for my people, but there are intruders everywhere now."

"Maybe he was lost," Brody suggested. "His horse didn't get skinny like that over the past few days." He stood up. "You really think an animal killed him?"

"It looks that way." Joseph took his hat off, reached inside, and smoothed a dent in its round top. He settled it back on his head, and got up. "Come help me get him in the wagon."

The lifeless weight of the body brought Brody's troubles to mind again, and he hesitated.

"Lift him higher," Joseph said.

Grunting, Brody struggled to hold on while they transferred him into the wagon.

"What do you think made the cuts? Something with only two claws?"

Joseph sat back down by the fire. "I have found more than one trap over the years with part of a paw caught in it. Found a whole leg one time."

"So, it could be a bear that got out of a trap," Brody said.

"Or maybe injured in a fight," Joseph added. He put a pot of coffee near the fire to reheat it. "There is something else worrying me."

"What is it?"

"My brother went missing out here a couple years ago. He has never turned up. I hope this bear, or whatever it is, has not started hunting men."

The top edge of the sun was sinking behind the mountain ridge. Brody looked at the gloomy woods and uneasiness crept over him. "I hope I don't ever see another man die like that again." He could not suppress a shudder. "Are we going to keep on trapping?"

"We will head to Fort Smith early in the morning," Joseph said. He eyed Brody over his tin cup before taking another sip of coffee. "Figured you might look forward to going to town. Young bucks need to stretch their legs. You have friends or family you want to see?"

Brody turned away so Joseph wouldn't see the anguish on his face. He shook his head.

Joseph was silent for a long moment. "You need an advance on your pay? I will take it off what is due."

"No, sir. I'll be fine."

Joseph grunted, and tossed the dregs of his coffee into the fire. It sizzled and steam rose into the air, then flames shot up again.

"Should be back before dark. Then we will just have to be real careful while running the traps." Joseph poured himself a fresh cup of coffee. "We can take the furs we have ready and drop them off at the Estes general store."

Joseph raised his voice. "Todd!"

Todd came out empty-handed. Joseph frowned. "Boy, where is the salt pork and beans?"

"Oh." The boy disappeared back into the shed.

Brody dreaded going to Fort Smith. He was wanted for murder, and it had been three months since Sarah had left him at the edge of town to make a decision whether to turn himself in to Judge Parker or leave and hope the vengeful Miller clan would tire of trying to hunt him down.

He left everyone he loved to keep them safe from the Millers, and now he was about to head back into the hornet's nest. Maybe if he asked Joseph to let him off at the edge of town, he could make his way to the stables unseen. If anyone might have word about his folks or Sarah, it would be the stable boy, Daniel.

Sarah. He missed her something awful. He hoped to see her again someday and maybe buy her a nice ribbon for her curly, black hair. He smiled. She might slap him again, but it would be worth it if she apologized with another kiss.

He sighed. As bad as he needed to stay away from Fort Smith, his desire to go was unbearably worse.

He walked out from camp, using the pale moonlight to find his marker, a cedar growing out of a crack in a boulder. Standing with his back to it, he stepped ten paces due north. After raking the leaves back, he located the slight mound over the small crate buried there.

Using his knife to dig, he removed enough of the dirt to lift off the lid. It had been months since he had opened it, so he checked inside for any critters that may be hiding.

He only had five of the double eagles left. He took one and put it in his pocket. "Thank you, Ames." He smiled as he covered the crate again.

When crazy Ames had found him on the mountain, Brody could never have imagined they would become best friends. The money he had gifted to Brody had gone a long ways in helping his momma and papa get back on their feet. He hoped life was treating Ames well in Crawford County.

After hiding the crate again, Brody brushed his pants off and went back to camp to have some supper. Joseph was working on one of their traps with a file. "What are you doing?"

Joseph put the file down and inspected his work. "We have had a critter tripping some of the traps without getting caught. I am filing the trigger on this one."

Brody leaned closer. "What will that do?"

After pushing the springs down, Joseph opened the jaws and set the trap. "See how the pan is completely flat?"

"Yes." Brody swallowed a bite of beans.

Joseph pointed but was careful to keep his finger out of the trap. "I filed a notch in the latch. It is set on a hair trigger now. If the pan moves at all, it will go off." He picked up a charred limb from the edge of the fire and barely touched the pan with it. *Snap!* "We will get that wise coyote with this one."

"You think it's a coyote that's been setting the traps off?"

Joseph nodded. "I feel certain of it. They like to dig them up." After pushing the springs down so the stick would fall out, he took the trap and put it away.

Todd wandered over and flopped down in the dirt. He watched Brody eat. Scooting across the ground, Todd looked over at Joseph. "Father, what would Flint's Indian name be?"

"Flint is not Indian."

"But neither was Mother," Todd said.

Joseph smiled at him. "She had no Indian name. Remember? She gave you your Christian name."

Todd turned to Brody. "Your name could be Eagle Eye."

Joseph laughed. "And yours should be Bird That Chitters."

"No, I'm Little Cub." The boy lost interest in the conversation, dug something out of his pocket, and eased closer to Brody.

Brody swallowed his last bite. "What are you doing?"

A big smile spread across Todd's face. He plopped a handful of marbles on the ground at Brody's feet, and then spun on his hind end. Brody picked his marbles up and waited. After a moment, Todd twisted back around with his hands cupped together.

He shook his fist, making the marbles rattle. "Hulla gulla. My hand's full. How many?"

Laughing, Brody said, "Six."

Todd opened his hands. "Five! Give me one of yours."

Brody surrendered one of his marbles.

"You are getting better," Todd said.

"I sure am," Brody said. "I might beat you this time."

They played several games and like always, Brody let Todd eventually win all his marbles back. Todd laughed each time he won.

"Time for bed," Joseph announced.

Todd frowned, gathered up his marbles, and dropped them in a canvas bag. "Can't I stay up and talk to Flint?"

"Not tonight," Joseph said.

Todd looked to Brody and shrugged. "Goodnight."

"Night, Todd."

The boy rushed off. Brody got up to wash out the supper plates. "Do you reckon that man had a camp near here?"

Joseph shook his head. "We have been running our trap lines and hunting for months now, and I have seen no trail signs but ours." He reached into his shirt and pulled out the bone necklace with the turquoise stone. His thumb circled the smooth surface. "It is a mystery and bothers me. Why would a man leave his camp with nothing but long underwear and a coat? Why would he leave on a horse with no saddle or bridle?"

A chill ran down Brody's spine. "He didn't have a weapon, either. Maybe he lost it when he was running."

"Hmmm… there are many possible reasons, but none that we can know for certain. Let us not borrow from trouble, and maybe he will not come looking for payment." He grinned, his white teeth shining in the firelight.

Brody picked up his rifle and inspected the stock. The crack had become wider and would break off completely if he didn't do something. He figured that was the reason he had missed the deer.

"Do you have any idea how to fix this?"

Joseph took the gun and wiggled the stock. "You could try wrapping some rawhide around it but it will not hold long. We can check on ordering one tomorrow in Fort Smith."

"That would take forever," Brody said.

"Maybe longer than forever." Joseph handed the Henry back to Brody. "Maybe you should make one."

"You think so?" Brody asked.

Joseph dug through a stack of cut firewood. He picked up one, looked at it for a second, and then tossed it back. Reaching down, he grabbed a thick piece of oak with a fork on one end. "This one. Here, hold this one next to it."

Brody took the wood and compared it to the broken stock. It was a little longer but about the same thickness. He held the forked end of the limb to his arm. He was surprised that it fit nicely and curved from the top of his shoulder and partway down under his armpit.

"Take your old one off," Joseph said. "Then you can see how to shape it."

"It's going to take a lot of work," Brody said.

"The tools are in the wagon." He smiled at Brody. "Better get started."

Joseph went into the camp-shed, but Brody stayed by the fire. He used Joseph's tools to remove the broken stock. Using his hunting knife, he started shaving the bark away. It would take a massive amount of work but he was willing to do it.

The campfire popped and snapped, sending tiny sparks into the air. A gentle breeze covered Brody with smoke, causing his eyes to burn and water. The cold night air made him shiver.

Keeping the limb tight against the top of his legs, he worked the blade of the knife against the rough bark. Slowly, the bark disappeared and the grain of the oak became visible.

The light from the fire lessened as it died, so he placed more wood on top. As he did, something moved in the brush. He listened intently but could not tell where the sound was coming from. The rustling stopped as suddenly as it had started.

The dire thought of a two-clawed bear slipping through the darkness sent prickles up Brody's back. The hairs on his neck stood tall, and he decided it was time for bed.

As he reached the shed, something howled in the woods, a deep throaty type of howl. Brody twirled around to face the direction of the sound. Within seconds, the door opened behind him and Joseph stepped out.

"Did you hear that?" Brody asked.

"Yes. Which way was it?"

Brody pointed. "What was it?"

Joseph shook his head. "I have not heard this animal's call before tonight."

Chapter Three

Carving an oak limb into a gunstock is hard. Doing it in a bouncing wagon is even harder but Brody did his best. Todd was sitting between him and Joseph. The boy leaned against his father and watched Brody. "Can I do it now?"

Turning the limb over, Brody started working on the other side. "Not yet."

He whittled on the new stock the whole trip. His fingers and hands ached but he kept at it. Joseph talked some, Todd chattered a lot, and Brody listened and spoke to them both but his attention stayed focused on the oak limb. Keeping his mind and hands busy helped to settle his nerves.

Joseph and Brody had run the lines at first light, then hitched up the wagon loaded with the body and tied the buckskin to the back. Brody had kept dragging his feet until Joseph was exasperated with him. "Come on, boy. You should be happy there is no skinning today, yet you seem as if a trip to town will kill you."

Joseph's comment had hit home. The Millers could be anywhere in Fort Smith. Ever since Brody accidently killed Doc Miller, then later took the ledgers proving Frank Miller was cheating his sharecroppers, the whole Miller clan was out for blood – his blood.

He couldn't just blend in with other folks. He raised his hand to trace the crooked burn scars that traveled from his eyebrow and down toward his cheekbone. Even a lock of his brown hair had come back in white. The day of his accident, nearly eight months ago, had left a permanent mark on him, in every way.

When he had tried to shoot a deer, a spark caused a bag of powder to explode in his face. It left him blind, hurting and in a terrible fix. But it also brought a crazy ex-slave to his rescue, and that man, Ames, became Brody's best friend.

That friendship also led to Brody and Ames becoming wanted for murder over the death of Doc Miller. This was why he should be headed back to the mountains and not into Fort Smith.

As they neared town, he let Todd whittle on the stock for a few minutes before putting the piece of wood away. Squeezing his hands into tight fists over and over eased the pain from all the carving. He brushed the wood shavings off of his lap. Reaching down to the floor, he picked up the big pieces, trying to clean out the wagon.

Underneath Joseph's seat, Brody spotted a hat, the exact thing he needed. "The sun is awful bright today. Can I borrow that old hat of yours?"

Joseph reached under the seat and pulled the crumpled hat out. "This old thing has no shape left at all. It will keep the sun off your face but it may keep you from seeing anything." He handed it over.

Brody slapped it against his leg and dust shot out. He put it on his head and pulled it down over his forehead. The brim on the old hat drooped and concealed most of his face. It couldn't have been better.

Joseph laughed. "Told you so."

Maybe he could go into town with the hat pulled low. If he was really careful, he might even see Sarah.

Reaching over to Todd, Brody tickled the boy's ribs. Todd giggled and squirmed, and jabbed at Brody's stomach. Joseph rolled his eyes at both of them and slapped the reins.

After taking the ferry, they arrived in Fort Smith. It seemed bigger, busier, and fuller. Brody kept his head down, making sure his face stayed hidden under the old hat. The wagon seemed to go unnoticed to everyone except for a few children. They waved, and Todd waved back.

Brody peered at Joseph from under the hat. "I've got a few things I need to do. Where can I meet y'all?"

Joseph stopped the wagon. "After I drop this poor fellow off, we will head on over to the general store. Look for a sign with E. M. on it. You can meet us there."

After jumping down from the wagon, Brody repositioned his hat.

"Do not be away too long," Joseph said. "Dark will catch us if we are not gone in an hour."

"Yes, sir," Brody said.

The wagon left and Brody crossed behind it. His thumping footsteps on the boardwalk mixed with others around him. It felt rude not acknowledging the people as he walked past, but he couldn't risk being recognized.

A storefront caught his attention. Signs covered its windows. Red and white ribbons decorated the doorway. Two well-dressed ladies came out smiling and talking about their purchases.

Brody glanced up at the storefront as he went inside. *The Boston Store.* A smaller sign on the wall had the words 'Fine Gifts For Fine People.' There were smooth fabrics and fancy hats with feathers. He was intent on finding something for Sarah and finally decided on a shiny, sky blue ribbon for her hair. A nice lady cut the ribbon for him and he paid her. He wanted to look around some more but after a fine dressed gentleman cast a suspicious look his way, Brody quickly exited.

Across the street was a smaller store. Inside, a counter filled with candy was near the front. He picked three swirled peppermint sticks and handed them to a man behind the counter. "I also need some rim-fire cartridges for a Henry."

The man stepped over to a shelf and picked up a box. "How many?"

"Two," Brody answered.

The storekeeper brought two boxes of shells over. Brody handed him some money.

The man pressed a button on the cash register and the drawer slid open. "Can I get you anything else today? A new hat, maybe?"

Brody bit his lip, and pulled the hat down lower. "No, thank you."

"Very good then." The man made change and handed Brody back several bills and some silver. "You're welcome back anytime."

Shoving the money in his pocket, Brody took his items, turned, and headed out the door.

He crossed the street and went in the direction of the stables. At the next corner he could see a girl coming toward him. His heart skipped several beats. He recognized Sarah's long black curls, and the way she walked like she always knew where she was going.

Leaning against a post, Brody waited on her. He wondered if she would even notice him since he had most of his face hidden under the floppy hat. He slipped the cartridges in his back pockets and waited.

He was admiring her graceful stride as she approached, and the sweet expression on her face as she greeted the people she passed, but then she stopped to talk to a boy. Brody snapped to attention.

He was maybe a couple of years older than Brody, about seventeen, and had wavy, reddish-blonde hair. He was well-dressed and looked clean, and he wore a red handkerchief around his neck.

Their muffled conversation was too far away to hear but it was clear they knew each other.

The boy smiled at Sarah and said something, causing both of them to laugh. He reached out and touched Sarah on the arm just briefly, but it was enough to set Brody's ears to burning. Finally, the conversation ended and Sarah continued toward Brody. She passed him by without the slightest glance.

"Sarah," Brody said.

She turned to look at him. "Yes?"

Brody tilted his head upward, allowing her to see his face.

She covered her mouth. "Brody?" Glancing around, Sarah strode past him and down between two buildings. She looked back and motioned.

He followed, and as soon as he got close, she grabbed his arm and pulled him behind a stack of crates.

"What are you doing here?" she demanded.

Brody grinned, "I just wanted to see you for a minute. I thought you might like to see me, too." He held out the blue ribbon.

Sarah placed a hand across her heart. "You got this for me?" On her mouth was the sweetest smile Brody had ever seen as she took the gift from his hand. "Oh, Brody, it's so pretty."

She leaned toward him and Brody puckered his lips, expecting a kiss of thanks.

She ignored his wrinkled lips and put her hand on his shoulder for a moment. "Of all the dumb things... Why are you even in town? The ribbon is beautiful, but you shouldn't be here. The Millers are out to get you and Ames."

Brody dug one of the candy sticks out. "I know." He held it out and waited for her to take it.

Sarah shook her head.

He let his arm drop.

"It's gotten worse, Brody. The law wants to question you about that murder and the Millers want you dead."

Brody's eyebrows rose. "That's about the way I remember it."

"What's new," she sounded put out, "is that you're now wanted for stealing horses, too."

"We didn't steal them." Brody thought she looked mighty pretty when she was riled up.

Sarah held her hand up to stop him from talking. Her hand was so fine and delicate-looking. It was the same hand she had slapped him with once, but then, followed it with a kiss. Brody felt his cheeks heating up.

"Brody Martin! Are you hearing a word I am saying?"

Brody startled. "Uhm… the Millers are after me?"

Sarah gave him a knowing look. "I said, the Millers now have a bounty out on you. Billy still says you killed his brother. Everything blew up after you left. Daniel got those ledgers to the judge, and a week later Billy lost his job and rumors started that he was in some trouble."

That got Brody's attention. He frowned. "He deserves worse for what he's done."

"They claim you and Ames stole their horses. They've put up personal reward posters around town. They're out for blood. Billy even tried talking to me several times after you left." She dangled her fingers in front of her mouth, making fun of Billy's bushy mustache.

"What did you tell him?" Brody didn't like the Miller's being close to Sarah.

The corners of Sarah's lips turned up, and she chuckled. "I told him the last time I saw you, you were beating a path south as fast as you could."

Brody pushed his hat higher and laughed. "Sarah, you're the best." He offered her the candy again.

Sarah's smile disappeared and she yanked his hat brim down. "It's a big mess. After Billy lost his job, one of the marshals found there weren't any bullet holes in Doc Miller's body, so he went back out to your farm. I'm guessing they didn't find enough evidence, but they still want you for questioning."

She paused and took the peppermint stick, only to put it in the pocket of her dress. "All they want to do is ask some questions."

Brody tilted his head. "What are you saying?"

"The Millers are out to kill you," she said. She reached out and laid her hand on his arm and squeezed. "I am worried, and I think you should talk to one of the marshals and tell him everything."

"They can't protect me from the Millers. Even if Billy isn't wearing a badge anymore, I bet he still has lots of friends that do, and I can't prove we paid for the horses."

Sarah dropped her hand and scowled. "Fine, don't listen to me, Brody Martin. You go ahead and get yourself killed." She stomped her foot and turned to leave.

Brody couldn't let her go like that. "Wait, Sarah! Don't be mad at me. Where you going?"

She stopped but kept her back to him. "I told Eli I would come and watch him shoot."

"Whose Eli? That dandy I saw you talking to on the boardwalk?" Brody couldn't quite hide his disdain.

Sarah faced him. The absence of any expression on her face worried him. "I have other things to do besides hiding in an alley."

"Well, who's this Eli to you?"

"A friend. He's entered the shooting contest, and I'm going to watch him practice."

Brody momentarily forgot Eli. "What shooting contest?"

"It's on the twentieth day of March I believe. A few merchants are offering prizes." She gave a tiny smile. "Eli's a good shot. I think he'll win."

Brody had never thought of himself as being the jealous type but at the moment it was eating him alive. "I was hoping we could talk for a while longer."

She looked at him long enough for him to feel his ears burning again. "If you weren't wanted, you could walk down the street with me. Maybe you could even go to the shooting contest with me instead of Eli."

Brody was dumbfounded. "You're going with Eli?"

Sarah walked out to the street and went around the corner. After a few seconds, she stuck her head back. "Oh, and your folks moved outside of town, south, at the edge of the prairie. They miss you a lot."

Before Brody could reply, she was gone.

There were few people on the street Brody walked down, and they were easily avoided. He was in turmoil. He alternated between fuming over Sarah and feeling elated that she had found where his family lived.

He yearned to see them, to hug Momma and Papa, and tell them all about his journey from the morning he snuck out to the foothills of the Devil's Backbone, to ending up in Indian Territory. Most of all, he wanted to explain why he stayed away, to tell them he wanted to keep them safe from the Millers.

When Brody finally found Joseph and Todd, they were in the middle of a heated discussion.

Todd had a death grip on the buckskin's lead and his voice rose with every word. "It's not fair!"

Joseph jerked the rope away. "I cannot believe you have done this."

"What did he do?" Brody took the boxes of shells out of his pockets and put them in the wagon.

Joseph threw up a hand. "The undertaker took the man's horse for burial payment, and while I was unloading the furs Todd went back over there and snuck the horse off."

Todd turned a stubborn and tear-streaked face to Brody. "I don't like that man. He won't treat Buck right."

"He is not our horse to take care of," an aggravated Joseph shot back. He shoved the lead rope into Brody's hands. "Return the horse while I consider tanning this boy's hide."

Todd crossed his arms. "Don't take him, Flint."

Leaning down, Joseph picked up Todd under the armpits and put him in the wagon. "Sit down."

"Go on," Joseph said to Brody. "We need to leave. The sun is moving faster than we are."

At that moment, a tall lanky man wearing a suit walked up to them. "Hold on there. Just what kind of trick are you trying to pull?"

"No, sir, Mr. Birnie," Joseph said. "No tricks. My boy has become a little attached to the horse."

The undertaker sniffed, casting a dark look at the defiant little boy. "I'll be taking my property back now."

Joseph took the rope from Brody and offered it to Mr. Birnie. Todd jumped up and opened his mouth, but a hard look from Joseph stopped him.

"How much?" Brody asked the undertaker.

The man took the lead from Joseph and jerked the horse away. The buckskin snorted.

"How much?" Brody repeated.

"For the horse?"

"Yes, sir."

The man's attention turned to the animal. "Well, this here is a twenty dollar horse."

Chuckling, Brody rubbed his hand along the buckskin's back. "He's skin and bones. Five dollars sounds more like it."

Joseph leaned back against the wagon and watched.

The undertaker brushed some dirt off the horse's leg. "It takes a lot of work to bury a man."

Brody raised his hat and scratched his head. "He's got that nasty wound on his neck, and by the time I get all the shed hair off him, his going to be skinnier by half again. I'll pay seven, just for your time in having to come down here. No one else is going to buy him and you won't get near that much selling him for dog scrap."

Mr. Birnie was looking intently at Brody's face. "Who gave you that scar?"

Chapter Four

R ealizing his mistake, Brody pulled the hat back down. "Ten. I'll give you ten. Last offer."

The undertaker's forehead wrinkled with surprise. He held his hand out and Brody paid him.

After the man had left, Joseph laughed at Brody. "I guess you are the proud owner of the poorest horse I have ever seen."

Brody handed Todd the lead. "I'm going to need help getting Buck healthy again. Know anybody who can help me?"

"Me!" Todd yelled. "I'll do it."

On the road back to camp, Brody worked on his stock. He tried to keep thoughts of Sarah and Eli out of his mind, but his jealously had not gone away. He was also worried about Ames. They were both wanted for horse theft and Ames had no idea. Maybe he should get word to him about the news. If Ames or one of his family members got caught with the horses, they would end up in jail, or worse.

Todd laughed from the back of the wagon. Brody looked and saw him leaning out and petting Buck's head each time the horse came close.

Joseph had been quiet for a long time. He held the reins with one hand and rubbed the bones on his necklace with the other. The bones were thin cross section circles, except for a turquoise stone that hung from the middle. They probably meant something special to Indians, but Brody couldn't imagine what it would be.

"You feeling all right?" Brody asked.

Pulling back on the reins, Joseph slowed the horses. "I was just thinking about the past and how trapping use to be."

Brody turned the oak stock over to carve on the other side. "How was it?"

"It was better," Joseph said. "Much better. More buyers. More money. It is hardly worth doing now."

"Why keep doing it?"

Joseph pulled at the leather strap on the necklace and then dropped it down his shirt. "It is what I know."

To keep his fingers from cramping, Brody stopped whittling. "I grew up on a farm. I miss it."

"Any brothers or sisters?"

"No, sir. It's just me and my folks."

Joseph glanced back at Todd, who was still busy with the horse. "His mother died four years after he came into this world. I am all he has. Well, my father is still alive, but he is of the old way. He only speaks Cherokee. My wife was a half blood and he never approved. He and Todd are the last of my family."

"Do you live close to Fort Smith?" Brody asked.

Transferring the reins to one hand, Joseph shoved his black hair away from his forehead. "We live in different places. Todd stays with me until winter. Friends keep him during trapping season but not this time. This is his first."

Brody wasn't sure what to say. He wanted to know more but was afraid to ask.

"Not the best," Joseph said, "but we work with what we have. When did you tell your parents we would be back?"

Brody's stomach twisted. He hated lying to Joseph. He had already made up his folks permission to hire on with Joseph, when in fact, his parents had no idea where he was or even if he was still alive. "End of March."

Leaning forward, Joseph snapped the reins. "You know, with that…" he lowered his voice, "man-killer sneaking around, I think we will pull out a little early. We can run the traps for another week or two and then break camp."

That news made Brody feel better. The thought of a bear or panther missing half a paw and liking the taste of human flesh gave him the willies. "Do you know what date it is?"

Joseph thought for a few seconds. "The man at the store said it is the tenth of March."

They rode in silence for a bit, listening to Todd chatter at Buck. Joseph cleared his throat. "The undertaker knew the man we brought in. Said he buried his wife three years ago."

"Did he know why the man was in the woods all the way in Indian Territory?"

"No. They came from Germany several years ago, to run sheep and make a fortune. He lost his farm instead. Then the wife took sick and died. He hired out for odd jobs to make ends meet. Mr. Birnie said he hadn't seen him for almost a month."

"That's a sad story."

Joseph slapped the reins, and the horses lengthened their stride. "Our path is not always a bright one." Leaning over, he looked at one of the wagon's wheels. "We have a loose wheel."

"Do we need to stop?" Brody asked.

Joseph sat straight again. "No. We can repair it before our next trip. All of the wheels need new seals and grease."

Brody snorted. "That sounds like a fun job."

They reached camp just before dark. After feeding the horses, Brody quietly stepped into the woods to put the money back in his wooden box. He uncovered the crate and opened the lid. As he dropped his money inside, someone said, "What's that?"

Every muscle in his body jumped, and Brody swung around.

Todd trotted to his side, went to his knees, and pulled at the wooden lid. "What's in there?"

Throwing a handful of leaves at Todd, Brody said, "Don't do that again."

"I scared you. I scared you." Todd wiggled at the waist and shook his head from side to side.

Brody couldn't help but laugh. "It's a treasure box." He opened the lid, allowing Todd to look inside.

Todd's jaw dropped. "Treasure!"

Brody took one of the coins from the box and handed it to him. "You can't tell anyone where it is."

Todd turned the gold coin over and over in his hand. "I won't," he whispered loudly. He carefully placed it back in Brody's palm.

After putting the money in the crate, Brody placed the lid back on top. "A wise friend of mine told me to never keep important things in camp."

"Why not?" Todd asked.

"Well," Brody said, "if we are out running traps and someone sneaks in the camp they could find it."

"And steal it," Todd added.

Brody nodded. "That's right. We should keep our valuables hidden."

Todd's eyes grew wide and a look of panic covered his face. "I'll be back." He sprinted away.

While trying to cover the little crate with leaves, Brody heard Todd rushing back.

"Wait!" Todd shouted. "I've got treasures." Rushing to Brody's side, he shoved the fox tail into his hands. "Put this in it."

After uncovering the box and taking the lid off, Brody placed it inside. Handing more things to Brody, Todd said, "And these too."

Brody took the items. "Are you sure? Your marbles? We can't play with them if they're hidden out here."

Todd nodded. "I'm sure."

Inspecting Todd's other treasures, Brody found one of the smallest flint arrowheads he had ever seen. Alongside the arrowhead was a nice sized white crystal. "Where did you get these?"

"Father gave 'em to me. They're my favorites. I don't want nobody stealing them."

Brody placed the things inside the box. "They'll be safe in here."

Todd leaned closer. "What treasures do you have? Anything from your father?"

Brody hesitated. He missed his papa and his momma something terrible. He had to find a way to see them, and the only way he could was if he managed to get back to Fort Smith. "All I have in the treasure box is some money and a map your father gave me."

Tilting his head to the side, Todd looked puzzled. "Nothing from your papa?"

Brody put the lid back on and started covering it. "Not in here. I've got my big knife, but I keep it with me."

"My father is a whole full blooded Indian." Picking up a stick, Todd held it out with one arm and pretended to pull a bowstring back with the other.

"I know that," Brody said.

"My ma was half Indian." Todd released his imaginary arrow and dropped the stick on the ground. "That makes me one and a half Indians."

Brody chuckled and was about to stand up to brush his knees off when Todd pushed him, causing him to lose his balance and fall.

"Hey, you little skunk. What did you do that for?"

"Your it!" Todd yelled as he ran back toward camp.

The next morning they got up early. The birds were just beginning to chirp and whistle in the trees.

Before setting out, Joseph took Brody by the arm. "I'm taking my shotgun today." He held up the double-barrel twelve-gage. "Since your gun is not working, I want you and Todd to stay close."

"Yes, sir." His comment reminded Brody he had left his new cartridges in the wagon. He retrieved the boxes, put them in the shed, and returned to Joseph's side.

Joseph pointed at Brody's head and grinned. "Do you need that floppy hat?"

Brody chuckled. "It's kinda cloudy. I don't think I'll need it."

They made a long walk on the rough trail to the west, checking and resetting traps along the way. In the bend of the trail, they found an empty trap that had been sprung.

Brody applied the stinky scent to a stick and handed it to Joseph. "Are you sure you won't tell me the secret recipe?"

"I could tell you but I would have to scalp you." Joseph laughed and then pushed the springs down and opened the jaws. Holding them with his foot and one hand, he adjusted the pan until it clicked. "I will show you how to mix it when we run out."

Joseph covered the trap with a thin layer of dirt and positioned some twigs and pebbles to guide the animal. If the stones were placed correctly, the animal would step right on the pan, triggering the trap.

On the way to the next setup, Brody kept Todd at his side. While working, Joseph always smoked. He swore the animals didn't mind and that it was only human scent that sent them running. The sweet smell from his cigar filled the air and clung to their clothes. It reminded Brody of his grandfather.

Todd struggled up a steep ridge. "Flint, how many deer have you killed?"

Pulling on Todd's arm, Brody helped him climb over some rocks. "Just a couple."

"How many squirrels?"

"Oh, I've killed a whole bunch of-"

"I killed a squirrel." Todd picked up a stick as they headed down the other side of the ridge. He held the limb up like a gun. "Father held the gun, but I shot the squirrel. Bang. We cooked him."

Brody laughed. "I bet he was proud of you."

Todd wacked a tree with the stick. "Have you killed any rabbits?"

"Yes, I-"

"My father shot six rabbits in one day. He's a good shot."

Joseph looked back, puffed up his chest and bumped it with his fist. Brody suppressed a chuckle. "He sure is," Brody said.

Todd swung the stick hard, over and over, causing it to make a whistling sound as it cut through the air. "He caught a bear last year. I don't like bears."

Brody stopped and waited while Joseph inspected a trap set. "I shot a bear last year."

Todd stopped swinging the stick. "Was it in a trap?"

"No, it was in my house," Brody explained.

"In your house?" Todd's stared at Brody in awe. Joseph raised an eyebrow.

He started out his tale with how his parents had gone on a trip and a friend had come to stay, and then they found the claw marks. By the time he got to where the bear was in the house and he shot it, both the trapper and the boy were staring at him in amazement.

Todd's mouth seemed as if it could never be closed again. "Are you telling a fib?" he finally asked.

"Nope," Brody said.

Joseph shook his head. "And I thought you were just a tenderfoot looking for his first job off the farm."

Brody laughed a little sadly. "Yes, sir, I was at that."

Joseph left the trail and disappeared into a thicket. Brody continued to finish up the set they were working on, keeping a watchful eye on Todd, and just as he was done, Joseph stepped back out on the trail.

He had the shotgun in a tight grip. "We're done here. Head back to the horses." After he spoke, Joseph pulled the bone necklace out of his shirt.

Todd tugged on Brody's sleeve. "But we've only caught one fox."

When Joseph got closer, he put his large hand on top of Todd's head and gently turned him around. "Remember where we left that fox on the way?"

"Yes, sir."

"I want to see if you and Flint can find him. I will follow right behind you." Joseph glanced behind him and then leaned close to Brody's ear. "There's something out here."

Chapter Five

B ack at the trapper shed, Brody kicked a pinecone back and forth with Todd while Joseph skinned out the fox. He hung the hide up, washed his hands, and then relaxed by the fire.

"I've got to work that hide," Brody said to Todd. "We can play some more later."

Todd ran to the shed. "I'm hungry." The door slammed behind him.

Poking holes around the edges of the hide, Brody started stretching it. He noticed Joseph staring toward the west. "What happened today?" Brody asked him.

Joseph got up and walked over. He came close and spoke quietly. "We will run the east trap line tomorrow. I do not think it wise to run the west one anytime soon."

Brody stopped working on the hide. "What's going on?"

"We had a number three set there with a drag chain and grapple. It is gone."

Traps had come up missing before, but they had always found them farther into the woods. "We'll find it."

"No, Flint. I mean it is gone. A coyote must have been in it. There is half a coyote lying there."

"Half?"

"Half," Joseph repeated. "The rest of it is gone, along with the trap and drag." He formed a circle with his hands. "There is a root this big around that is pulled up. It is all scarred where the hooks on the grapple caught it and I saw gouges in the ground and a sapling as big as my wrist pulled clean out."

"What could have done that?"

Joseph shook his head slowly. "I do not know. Something big took off with part of that coyote and the trap. Those drag hooks dug in and whatever had it, just kept on going."

Brody dreaded asking, but did anyway. "Bear?"

"Maybe. But no bear sign, so maybe not." He paused. "My father would say it was Tsul 'Kalu."

Brody wrinkled his eyebrows. "What?"

"An old Indian legend," Joseph explained. "A giant hairy man-creature."

It was Brody's turn to raise an eyebrow.

Joseph chuckled at him. "It is just an old legend. I am thinking it is only a rogue bear. We will avoid that area and work the east for a while." He patted Brody on the shoulder. "We will be fine. We just need to be careful."

"You think it's the same thing that killed that man?"

Joseph shrugged. "It happened in the same area. I would have to believe so." He pointed at the fox skin. "When you get done, come and get some food."

Brody stretched and scraped the hide. He hated bears, though he had a feeling Joseph didn't believe it was a bear. He finished working on the fur, cleaned up, and then ate with Joseph and Todd. After that, he worked on his gun stock. Now he had an urgent reason to get it finished. There was a killer in the mountains.

The next morning, Brody attached his homemade Henry stock. It took several tries to get the bottom and top grooves to fit the brass extensions correctly. Once he had it shaped just right, it didn't wobble at all. He marked the spot where the bolt needed to be and used Joseph's hand-drill to make a hole through the wood. After tightening the bolt, he put the wood screw back in the bottom and held the gun at arm's length. He admired his work.

The new one did not resemble the old one at all. It was longer, lighter in color, not as smooth, and curved around his shoulder. The brass butt plate wouldn't fit the new stock, so Brody left it off.

While walking by, Joseph stopped for a look. "Not bad. You should shoot it a few times. Try hitting that old stump down there."

Brody spotted the stump he was talking about. It looked to be about forty strides away. The wide base would be hard to miss. After loading the gun, he leaned against a tree, took aim, and shot. A chunk of dead bark flew into the air.

"Good shot," Joseph said.

Todd came running out of the shack. "What are you shooting?"

"Flint killed a stump," Joseph said. "Run down there and see where he hit it."

Todd sprinted in the direction Brody had shot. Standing the gun upright, Brody made sure it wasn't pointed at him.

After reaching the stump, Todd inspected it for a moment, then, shouted back, "He hit it here in the middle."

"Very nice," Joseph said to Brody. "Try that fallen tree. That is about seventy steps."

Brody waited until Todd was back at their sides. He aimed at the dead tree. The butt of the gun stock cupped his shoulder nicely. He fired, but didn't see where the bullet hit.

Todd took off toward the tree. Once he had reached it, Todd looked it over, checking for the bullet hole. "I don't see it."

"To your left a little," Brody said loudly.

After looking again, Todd shrugged. "You missed." He came running back.

"You did not adjust your sight," Joseph said.

"I aimed higher," Brody said.

To Brody's surprise, Joseph reached over and raised the rear sight and adjusted it a tiny bit. "Did no one show you how to do this?"

While inspecting the mechanism, Brody shook his head. "I didn't know it could be done."

"You will shoot even better," Joseph said. "Try some more later."

"Thanks, Joe." Brody checked his gun and discovered he only had a few bullets left. He ran to the shed and grabbed one of the new boxes and put it in his pack.

Joseph climbed onto his horse's saddle. "Let's go check that east line."

"Can I ride Buck?" Todd asked Brody.

"Sure can," Brody said. He helped Todd on the buckskin and then got on Joseph's other horse.

Brody was excited about running the east line. The land was flatter, with small rises, not the big cliff and ridges that lay to the north and west. They could ride the horses the whole way, letting them do most of the work. He just wasn't sure how well Buck would hold up under a wildcat like Todd.

Over the next few days, Brody worked hard. He took care of the furs, oiled his new gun stock with rendered deer fat the way Joseph instructed, and even managed to squeeze in a little time for shooting. Since he had learned how to use the rear sights, Brody was hitting dead on at fifty steps and was ready for longer shots.

Brody couldn't get his folks off his mind. When he was scraping hides, his body went through the motions, but his mind was racing down different paths, trying to figure out a way to see his momma and papa. There had to be a way to sneak around Fort Smith and find where his parents were living. Maybe he could slip in after dark and leave before daylight. Maybe Sarah would get Daniel to be a lookout for him.

He couldn't chase thoughts of Sarah and that boy she was talking to out of his mind, either. The more he thought about her going to the shooting contest with Eli and his fancy get-up, the more his dander got up. He got so frustrated that he angled the scraper too hard and cut completely through the hide. He groaned.

He threw the scraper down and thumped his fists on his thighs. He made up his mind. He was going to the contest, and he was going to see his folks.

There were no more missing traps, or signs of the bear or any other legendary creatures. Trapping fell back into a familiar routine, but Brody and Joseph kept a close watch on Todd. The boy stayed busy helping with Buck. With lots of care and extra food, the horse was gaining weight and getting stronger.

Brody had been notching days out on a stick, so when the eighteenth day arrived, he couldn't wait any longer. He had to ask Joseph about going into town.

After supper, Joseph relaxed by the fire and smoked a cigar. Todd rambled around the edge of camp scouting up pinecones and acorns to throw in the flames. Brody sat by Joseph and cleared his throat.

"Joe, I need a favor."

"What is it?" Joseph puffed smoke into the air with his words.

"I need to… Well, I was wondering…" Brody's flubbed words frustrated him. "Can I leave for a couple days?"

The tip of Joseph's cigar glowed red. "What are you planning?"

"It's… Well, there's this shooting contest at Fort Smith."

Joseph tapped the cigar against the log. "A turkey shoot? That is a long trip just to shoot your gun a few times."

Brody's shoulders slumped. He had been afraid the conversation would go this way. "Yes, sir."

"There has to be another reason," Joseph suggested.

"No, sir." Brody took out his knife and picked a piece of wood to whittle on.

The crackling of the fire was the only sound between them. Brody desperately tried to think of another way to persuade the big Indian to let him go. Finally, Brody realized there was no other way. "It's a girl," he confessed.

Joseph's forehead wrinkled and he sat up straight. "Is that the truth?"

"Yes, sir."

A racket behind the shed heralded the arrival of Todd with an armful of pinecones. He threw one into the fire and watched the flames spread into it.

Flicking his ashes again, Joseph said, "A girl. You want to enter a turkey shoot to make yourself big for a girl."

"Her name is Sarah," Brody said defensively.

"Who's Sarah?" Todd asked.

"Go inside and get ready for bed," Joseph said to Todd. A deaf man could have heard the irritation in his voice.

Todd did not argue and quickly went to the shack, singing, "Flint's got a girl! Flint's got a girl!"

Brody figured Joseph would have laughed and teased him about trying to impress a girl. Just a few days ago, he was encouraging him to spend time in town, so now he was a little confused and a lot worried about Joseph's reaction.

Joseph threw the butt of his cigar into the flames, leaving a trail of smoke as it tumbled through the air. "You heard of Billy the kid, right? He is bad. Done bad things. But he is smart and sneaky."

"Yes," Brody said.

"He has been caught. I read about it while we were in town. He tried to hide but they got him, and you can bet that fellow, Jesse James, will get caught too."

Brody's heart sped up. He knew his face must be turning red.

Reaching in his pocket, Joseph removed a piece of paper. He unfolded it and held it up for Brody to see. "You can not keep hiding."

Brody took a deep breath. It was the reward poster Sarah had told him about.

Chapter Six

"They will find you. Mr. Birnie will remember a boy of fifteen years, and a big scar on his face, buying a skinny horse off of him." Joseph shook the paper. "This means you have people looking for you. Bounty hunters, lawmen, and every poor soul who wants quick money."

The center of Brody's body began to shake as his nerves took over. "I didn't do those things."

"That does not matter," Joseph said. "You lied to me. Your real name is Brody. Worse than that, the type of people who try to collect reward money, they are not the friendly type. They do not care where all of their bullets go, just as long as they get the person they are looking for." Joseph sighed heavily. "You have put me and Todd in real danger."

"I am sorry." Brody rubbed his hands through his hair. It was the truth and he felt horrible about it. "I am so sorry. I would never want anything to happen to you or Todd."

"I know," Joseph said. He chewed his bottom lip and looked at the poster for a few seconds. "Bad people do bad things. I have spent a lot of time with you and I know you are not bad, not even a little bit. I know you care about Todd, and I believe what you are telling is truth to me."

"It's the truth. We didn't steal anything and I didn't kill that man. Well, I kinda did by accident. He was trying to run down my friend so I shot his horse and the man got killed. Billy Miller is his brother and now he's after me."

"They are bad people," Joseph said. "Just like I said, bad people do bad things."

"Yes, sir. They've done some terrible things."

Joseph stared at him for a moment. "Is there a girl and a turkey shoot, or were you just running off?"

"There is," Brody said. "I also needed to warn my friend that the Millers are calling us horse thieves."

"I and the little cub have grown to care about you," Joseph said. "I do not want the evil of bad men to fall on you. You must find a way to fix this. Go to your lawmen."

"I can't. I found some ledgers and papers that proved Billy had been cheating folks. I sent them to the judge and Billy lost his job. Even though he's not a deputy anymore, I'm sure he still has friends that are lawmen and they won't believe me." Brody paused. "Billy and his son want me dead, and I don't know how to stop them."

Joseph turned the poster around and held it up. "Your name is Brody Martin. Hiding and pretending to be someone else is no way to live."

"What should I do?"

Standing up and then brushing his pants off, Joseph looked down at him. "You should talk to Marshal Reeves. He is a good man. He lived with my family for a while when he was younger. I can go with you."

Brody thought about the offer. "I'm afraid the Millers would be looking for you then." He paused. "And I have a few things to do."

Joseph was grave. "This will haunt you the rest of your life. If you do not take care of it, you will never have peace again."

Brody rubbed the scar above his eyebrow slowly and watched the fire dance. "I need some peace. I need things back to normal but they never..." His eyes began to water and he cleared his throat. "I've had the jitters about seven months. I just want...." He couldn't find the right words. His family, a girl, a place to call home again… maybe that was it.

He told Joseph everything that had happened since that day he snuck off to find food for his family, until the day that Joseph had stopped at the stable and offered to hire him on for this season.

After he finished his tale, the trapper was quiet for a long time. Finally, he said, "I have been wrong about you. You are no tenderfoot farmboy." He nodded slowly. "Go see your girl and your friend. Come back in two days and we will break camp. Then, we will go see Mr. Reeves and try to straighten this crooked path."

Brody stood. Joe was right. It was time for something to change. "Yes, sir. I will."

Joseph held the reward poster out and Brody reached for it. Before he could take it, Joseph dropped it in the fire. The flames began to eat the edges. The paper burst into yellow and orange flames, and then curled into a black, fragile ash.

The big trapper stood up and stretched. He reached over and clasped a hand on Brody's shoulder, then strode toward the shed. The matter seemed to disappear along with the ashes of the reward poster. It made Brody's chest tight with emotions. Joseph had accepted him and all of his problems.

He got up early the next morning, feeling as if a weight had lifted off his shoulders. He went to the hidden crate, smiling when he saw Todd's treasures, and drew out the folding money and double eagles. He wasn't sure what he would need for the contest or his trip to find Ames.

Back at camp, he brushed Buck and placed a blanket on his back. The horse was filling out nicely and was good-natured enough to put up with Todd's antics. The hair was growing in white where his neck had been slashed. Buck reached around and lipped Brody's sleeve, making him chuckle. "You can't be hungry again, I just fed you."

Todd raced over to Brody and grabbed his waist, "I want to go, too." Joseph was grinning when he came up and peeled the protesting boy off of him.

"If you went with Brody, I would not have my fierce cub to guard the camp." Todd stopped struggling to consider this, then nodded and stepped back. Brody looped Buck's lead over his neck and tied the loose end to the other side of his halter. He needed to find a real outfit for his horse, soon.

Joseph laced his fingers together and formed a cup. He leaned down and Brody put his boot in it. Joseph grunted as he heaved Brody up. "You are so heavy now you hurt my back. You better learn to mount like us Indians."

"Aww, Father, you don't even ride bareback anymore without fussin'," Todd pointed out.

"Little cub, I can still leap on a running horse using only one hand." Joseph frowned fiercely in mock indignation. "Just not today."

All three of them laughed.

Joseph handed up the Henry rifle. Brody was surprised to see a leather sling attached to it. "You can borrow this until you get back."

"Thanks, Joe."

The boy begged again to go with him.

"I'll just be gone two days," Brody promised.

"I want you to hurry," Todd said emphatically.

"I will."

Joseph handed the old floppy hat to Brody. "Keep it pulled down low."

"Yes, sir," Brody said.

"I put some jerky, beans, and apples in the saddle bag," Joseph said.

Brody reached over and shook his hand. "Thank you. I'll be back soon."

Removing his bone necklace, Joseph offered it to him. "I want you to have this."

"I can't," Brody said.

Joseph forced the necklace into Brody's hand. "Take it. It will bring you good luck."

Brody hesitated.

"Take it," Joseph said again.

Placing the necklace over his head, Brody tucked it inside his shirt. "I'll keep it safe."

Joseph smiled. "You will do fine." He picked up Todd and slung him over a shoulder. Todd squealed and kicked. "Some dark clouds are coming. You better get across those creeks before it rains."

Brody kicked Buck's sides and headed for Arkansas.

He kept Buck at a steady ground-eating pace. After a few hours, he stopped to eat some deer jerky and let Buck graze.

When he tried to climb back on Buck, the blanket slipped off, and Brody decided to take Joseph's suggestion to mount like an

Indian. He grabbed a handful of mane, crouched a bit, and then sprang up, trying to swing a leg over the top of the horse. After thumping his boots into Buck's ribs for the fifth time, and several mournful looks from the horse, Brody decided he better figure something else out.

A steep bank was next to the trail. He led the horse over and stopped him next to the incline. Climbing up, Brody was able to position the blanket and then throw his leg over Buck's back.

Dark clouds in the west were rapidly forming. While the front edge was a fluffy gray, everything behind it was nearly black. Minutes later, thunder rolled and the temperature began to drop.

Brody didn't even have time to pull out his slicker. There were no pitter-patter drops of warning. The sky opened. Within seconds, a wall of rain crashed down.

Brody pulled the hat tightly on his head and stopped under a big tree, but the heavy drops found him anyway. Putting on his waterproof poncho now seemed pointless, but he didn't want his rifle getting any wetter, so he wrestled it on.

Soon the thunder became fainter as the front moved eastward. The rain had set in, and didn't look like it would be stopping any time soon. Having been soaked to the bone, he decided he might as well keep going.

Nudging Buck's sides with his heels, Brody headed down the trail. His horse felt strong under him and walked through the rain and mud without complaint.

They continued for another few hours and so did the rain. A cold wind chilled Brody and he began to shake. Holding his arms against his stomach, he curled forward on Buck's neck, trying to block the damp breeze.

"Howdy," a gruff voice said.

Shuddering all over, Brody almost fell off his horse. He had not noticed another rider coming toward them.

The man talked loudly to be heard over the sound of the rain. "You all right?"

Brody looked at him from under the hat. "Hi, mister..." He couldn't finish. The big man was wearing an eye-patch and a large tin star peeked out of his raincoat. "Hi, m-m-mister," Brody stuttered again, grateful for the obscuring rain between them.

The man pulled a flask from inside his jacket. It clinked and then scraped against his badge. "You having any trouble?"

"No, sir."

After taking a swig, the man put the flask back. "You a trespasser? Or are you supposed to be over here?"

"I took my new horse out exploring. When it started raining, I got a little turned around."

"Turned around so bad, you crossed the river without knowing it?"

"I d-d-idn't cross the river, sir. I'm supposed to be in Crawford County."

"You didn't see the iron post, marking the border?"

"No, sir. I'm s-sorry."

"Keep on this road for a mile and then cut northeast," the man said. "Get back in Arkansas where you belong."

"Yes, sir. Th-thanks."

The fellow nodded and continued on his way. As he disappeared into the rain, he started to sing. Prickles ran all over Brody's skin as he realized how close he had come to being caught.

Kicking Buck's sides, Brody brought him to a trot. He couldn't risk meeting any more lawmen on the road.

He was thankful when the rain slacked off and the sun finally reappeared. Before reaching Fort Smith, he left the road and turned Buck northward. Coming up on the river, he turned and followed it. His plan was to stay on the edge of the waterway as it curled above town. It would take him right into Crawford County where he could find Ames.

Half a mile later, he finally stopped shivering. A swollen feeder creek came into view, and the brown water stained the river as it emptied into it. There wasn't any way around the tumbling rapids.

He patted the horse's soggy neck. "Are you ready, Buck? We're already wet and cold, and we better go now. It's only going to get worse as the creeks rise."

This would be a true test for the buckskin. Brody could see the danger of being swept down the creek and into the river. He decided he would try it if Buck was willing. If the horse refused, they would have to set up camp by the river and wait.

After wrapping the saddlebag and his knife in the horse blanket and pulling a hard knot in the rope, he tied it around his waist. He made sure the Henry was tight in the sling on his back and under his slicker. Easing the buckskin down to the water, he wrapped his fingers in Buck's mane.

Reaching back, Brody slapped him on the hip. The horse stutter stepped, nodded his head, and snorted. Brody swatted him again and squeezed with his legs. Buck jumped forward, splashing into the river. Within seconds, the horse was swimming.

Brody dropped the reins and held onto Buck's neck with both hands. The cold water took Brody's breath away. Floating on his stomach, he tried kicking his feet but his boots kept hitting the horse's back. The current pushed them downstream but Buck's legs churned hard.

They came closer and closer to being swept into the Arkansas River. Brown water washed over the horse's neck and covered

Brody's face. He strangled and coughed, raising his head to see a huge log sweeping towards them. Brody screamed, "Go, Buck!"

Chapter Seven

B uck laid his ears back and surged forward. The log barely missed them. Buck's legs churned, and soon his hooves touched the bottom near the opposite bank.

Brody sank back down on Buck's back as he struggled out of the water. The horse was blowing hard after all the effort. Brody leaned forward and hugged his wet neck. "You are amazing!"

The buckskin had turned out to be ten times better than Brody had expected. He unrolled the soaked horse blanket to ring it out as best he could, and wrapped it around his body. The knife went back in its sheath, and the Henry was still safe on his back. He breathed a prayer of thanksgiving that the leather saddlebags had kept most of the food and grain dry.

After another hour of uncomfortable traveling, he started to warm up a bit. Crawford County was big and he knew locating Ames would be difficult, but he was sure hoping to find him before dark.

Up ahead, he noticed a black man throwing hay out of a wagon. Dozens of cows crowded around, pushing each other in an attempt to get at the feed.

"Hey, mister. You know where Ames lives?"

The man threw another armload of hay. "Ames?"

"He goes by Ames or Amos," Brody explained.

"Sure don't," the man said.

"Thank you anyway." He continued on the muddy trail. Buck slipped but recovered. His hooves squished with each step. They came to a washout in the road. The water had reduced to a trickle but had left a knee-deep ditch behind. Buck jumped it without hesitation. Brody rubbed the horse's shoulder. He was the best horse anyone could ever ask for.

Bright sunlight continued to warm Brody's skin, and his clothes felt a bit drier. A bumblebee flew within a foot of his face, stopping and hovering for a moment before buzzing away.

At a crossroad, he happened upon an elderly couple checking their fences. They had not heard of Ames, so Brody kept going. Just before dark, he saw a young colored fellow chopping firewood. He asked him about Ames, and the man pointed down a rutted out wagon track.

As Brody rode onto the property, a yellow dog rushed up to him, barking. Buck snorted, but calmly kept trudging across the wet ground. A white-washed house was to the left of the track. Smoke rose from its stone chimney. A rocking chair sat on the front porch. To the side of the house was a large tarp stretched between two trees.

Mary came outside. Brody had not seen her since the night he and Ames saved her from the Millers. She had the same sweet smile and it warmed Brody's heart.

When she recognized him, she hollered with excitement. "Brody! It's so good to see you."

He got down and tied Buck to a post with a ring in it. "It's good to see you too." He hugged her.

She patted him on the back. "What are you doing all the way up here? Get inside, you're wet as all get out."

"Not nearly as wet as I was."

After closing the door, Mary brought him a towel, then set his gun and saddlebag in the corner. "How have you been?"

"Good." He rubbed his hair vigorously. "I've been trapping in Indian Territory."

"Oh, my." Mary stifled a snicker, as he handed her the towel back.

Brody looked at her questioningly.

"Your hair." She left the room for a minute.

Brody looked around. A large stove was in the corner. Next to it was a sack of potatoes. A round table was close to the kitchen, and a lantern was set in its middle. Two doorways could be seen from the main room. Brody guessed the home had two bedrooms. It was a massive improvement from the one room cabin Mary had been living in on the Miller's property.

She came back out and handed Brody a comb. "Where's everybody?" Brody asked, flattening his damp hair down with the comb.

"Anna and Luke are visiting a friend." Mary went to the kitchen. "You want a glass of water, or how 'bout some hot coffee."

"I'd take a cup of coffee, and thank you much." Brody sat at the table. "Where's Ames?"

Mary stoked the fire, and put a pot on the stove. She came back to the table and sat across from him.

A nice set of curtains covered the front window. They looked brand new. The wood floor was squeaky clean and there wasn't a cobweb anywhere to be seen.

"This is a really nice place," Brody said.

"Thank you," she said absently. Her face was fuller. She looked to have gained some weight, but worry wrinkles had found a home between her eyebrows. Brody had the feeling she was thinking hard on something.

"Amos isn't doing too well," she finally said.

Brody tensed up. "What's wrong?"

After rubbing her face, Mary sat back in the chair. "I think he spent too much time up on that mountain."

"Is he all right?"

She gave a tired laugh. "He's a little strange sometimes."

Brody nodded. "I remember." *Is ye Union, or is ye Confederate?*

Mary stood, went to the window, and looked out. "He won't even stay in the house anymore. Most nights he sleeps under that old tarp out there. Sometimes, I hear him yelling about Yankees."

Brody nodded. "Miss Mary, the war was hard on him."

Mary came back to the table. "And being alone all those years. That was hard on him too."

"He never thought he'd find you and Anna, again."

"He's restless, Brody, real restless, like he can't get settled. I'd appreciate if you would talk with him."

"Sure I will. I'd like to stay the night if it's no bother."

Bending over, Mary hugged Brody and kissed him on the top of his damp head. "You're welcome anytime. You know that." She went to the kitchen and poured some coffee. "How long are you staying?"

"Just for tonight. I'm headed to Fort Smith tomorrow."

Mary looked shocked. "Lord help, boy, why on earth would you be going to Fort Smith? Right into that nest of Millers, and the law looking for you, too?" She shook her head.

Thoughts of Billy and Frank shooting at him from the crossroads came to mind. Was he making a mistake going into a town where he was wanted?

But he sure missed his momma and papa, especially after Miss Mary's hospitality. A pang of homesickness hit him. "I really want to see my folks. My momma doesn't even know if I am still alive."

Mary sighed. "I spent years not knowing if I still had a husband. I understand your feelings, Brody. I don't like it, but I understand." She set a cup of hot coffee on the table.

Brody thought about the shooting contest. Maybe it was too big of a risk. There would be a lot of townsfolk coming just to watch, and some of the shooters might even be lawmen.

He could just slip into town and see his folks, and get word to Sarah he wasn't going to enter. That should make her happy. Then he pictured Sarah giving Eli a big kiss when he won the shooting contest, and he knew he had to beat that no-good coyote.

He took the cup Mary had set down, and sipped from it, resolving not to mention the turkey shoot. "Hmm, that's good. Oh, I almost forgot. I need to take care of my horse and get my things dry."

Pointing toward the back of the house, Mary said, "There's a corral in the back, and a little shed." She laid a hand on his arm as he started up. "Drink your coffee first, and tell me why on earth you were over in Indian Territory."

<hr>

After taking Buck behind the house, Brody gave him some feed and rubbed him down with an empty gunny sack. He rubbed the scar on the gelding's neck, and pulled an apple out of his pocket. Buck bit off half of it.

"You done good today, Buck. The only horse I've ever had was a little pony called Tater. He was small and lazy as a mule, but he was mine. I gave him up to a little black boy named Daniel. Tater could never have done what you did today."

Buck nuzzled his hand, leaving a trail of apple slobber. Brody wiped it off on his pants and chuckled. "You're just as messy, though." He patted him one more time. "Rest up. We've got a lot of traveling to do tomorrow."

Back inside, he asked Mary if he could dry out his belongings in front of the hot stove. She helped him lay out his blanket, and offered a rag so he could wipe down his gun and knife. Mary was still worried that he might be recognized in Fort Smith, so Brody put the hat on and showed her how it disguised his scar.

"Well, you keep that hat pulled low, and keep your head down when folks are around." She took a checkered cloth off the black skillet on the stove. "How 'bout a bite of cornbread to hold you 'til supper?"

His stomach growled at the thought. "Yes, ma'am."

She handed a piece to him and stood there for a moment. "I wish you would take Amos with you."

"Ma'am?"

"He's lost that sparkle in his eyes. I think it would do him good to spend some time with you. Besides, we need things to settle down a little around here. Anna is going to have a baby."

"You're going to be a grandmother?" Brody asked.

Mary's eyes sparkled, and a huge smile lit up her face. "Finally."

The dog barked outside. Mary went to the window and pulled the curtain back. "Amos is home."

"Who in der?" a loud voice called out.

"Ames!" Brody jumped up from the table.

"Come on out," Ames threatened.

Mary opened the door and stepped out, Brody hard on her heals. "Amos, put your gun up! Come, look who's here."

Brody stepped onto the porch and saw Ames in the yard. He was holding his musket. He was still the tall, lean man Brody remembered. His beard had grown back in more white than gray, but not nearly as long.

"Well, I say." Ames smiled. "My lil' feller."

Coming across the yard in a run, Brody skidded to a stop in front of the man that had rescued him in the foothills of the Devil's Backbone.

They hugged and Ames slapped him on the back over and over.

"Where ya been, Brody?"

Letting go of Ames, Brody stepped back, grinning like a fool. "I've been working and trapping."

"Get dem papers ta Parker?"

"Yes, sir. I hear you're going to be a grandpa." They walked to the cabin, sometimes both talking at once.

Mary cooked while Ames and Brody swapped stories. Soon they were eating venison, with cornbread and mashed potatoes, and generous helpings of apple pie. "Miss Mary, I think I've done died and gone to heaven. We sure don't eat this well at camp."

"Oh, shaw, Brody, you go on now. It's nothing to fuss over."

Ames winked at Brody. "Don't believe her none. Anna's got folks all over da county buy'n dem pies."

Mary looked pleased as she gathered up the plates. "Y'all just sit there and visit while I tidy up."

Ames licked his fork clean and passed it over to Mary. "Me and Luke done broked da ground all up. It's ready fer plantin'. Just needs ta warm up some more."

Brody leaned back in his chair. "I didn't expect this cold rain today."

"It gonna set da crops back fer sure."

"Have you heard anything about the Millers?" Brody asked.

Ames shook his head. "Nope."

"Billy got in some sort of trouble because of those ledgers. The law still wants to talk to us about what happened to Doc Miller, but I think they suspect we didn't do it on purpose."

Mary came over and refilled the coffee cups. "That's good news."

"Yes." Ames said. "Dat is some kind of fine news."

"But the Millers are still claiming murder on us, and the law wants us for horse theft," Brody said.

Ames put his cup down so hard, coffee splashed out. Mary frowned and used her dishcloth to blot it up. Ames ignored her, his faced clouded with anger. "How so?"

"Those horses we paid Frank for the night we went to his house," Brody explained. "The Millers claim we stole them. They have a reward out for us."

Ames blew out a long breath. "Dem Millers is a fine bunch of folks, ain't dey?"

Mary washed the same spot on the table over and over again. "I knew Frank wouldn't give up."

"I know you paid him," Brody said to Ames. "But, we don't have a way to prove it."

Mary sat next to them and looked to Brody. "Is the law still after Amos for that old murder the Millers put on him?"

"I haven't heard anything else about it but I'd have to guess so. Billy's after us hard. He lost his job."

Ames let out an angry growl. "Hope he get a lot worse den dat."

"Mary, you said Luke and Anna are at a friend's. They aren't using those horses, are they?"

"No," Ames said. "We needed mules ta work da crops so I traded dem horses."

Brody was relieved. "Good. You don't need to be seen with them."

Ames leaned forward, "It still a big ol' mess, ain't it?"

"I'm going to Fort Smith to see my folks, and maybe Sarah. After that, I'll head back to Indian Territory to break camp and pull the traps, and then Joe's taking me to talk to a marshal."

Ames frowned. "I don't know 'bout dat."

"It'll be okay," Brody said. "Joe says this marshal is a good man."

"Who dis Joe?"

"Joseph Wolf. He's a trapper in Indian Territory, and he hired me on. He's a real nice man. He's taught me a lot and I trust him."

The dog barked outside, and Ames jerked upright. He became fixated on the front window. "Dey somebody sneakin' round."

He jumped up in such a rush, his chair toppled back and to the floor. He headed for the door, snatching his musket up on the way.

Brody rose up to follow. "Ames, what's happening?"

Ames was already gone. Brody started after him, but Mary grabbed his arm.

"Ain't nobody out there." Her voice was harsh.

Ames hollered at someone. A few second later, he crossed in front of the door and limped down the steps, stumbling on the last one so hard, he almost fell. He recovered and raised his fist in the air. "Cowards!"

Brody stepped outside and watched him disappear into the fading light. "Ames. Are you hurt? Get back in here."

Mary came to stand beside him. "He's not hurt. His bad leg has just been giving him some trouble."

Brody looked at the tears in her eyes. "Shouldn't I go after him?"

"Ain't nothing you can do," Mary said, her voice thick. "Not while he's like that." She patted at her eyes with her dishcloth. "He's getting worse, too." She turned back into the house.

Brody stared into the gloom, and thought he could see a vague shape crouched down among the trees off beside the house. He shook his head, the day's joy turned to sorrow.

Mary called from inside, "You can sleep in Luke and Anna's bed. They won't be back until tomorrow, and I put fresh linens on it today."

Brody walked back inside with a heavy step. "I wish…."

She hugged Brody. "Shush, now. He'll come around and be all right by morning. You can talk to him then." Mary went to the bedroom door. "Good night. I'll see you in the morning."

"Good night, Miss Mary."

Brody waited up for a while but Ames didn't come back inside. He finally went to bed and did his best to fall asleep. After hours of trying, he decided to get up and check on Ames.

A faint glow came from the canvas tarp. The wind blew the flap gently. Each time it flopped, he could see Ames sitting inside, staring at a sputtering lantern. As Brody approached, the yellow hound dog growled.

Ames sprang up, gun in hand. "I'll kill ye."

Chapter Eight

Heart thumping, Brody backed away with raised hands. "It's me, Ames."

After taking a few steps, Ames stopped. "Dat's my family. You stay back."

"Ames, nobody is going to hurt your family."

"Nobody gonna hurt my family," Ames repeated.

Brody squatted down and rested his forearms on his knees. "It's okay. Everything's fine."

Ames stared hard at Brody. "Everything fine."

Brody held his breath.

Ames nodded once, then turned around. He limped back inside the canvas tent and sat.

Cautiously, Brody walked closer and waited by the opening, but Ames didn't say anything else. "Come inside," Brody finally suggested. "Come in and go to sleep."

Cupping his face with one hand, Ames shook his head and rubbed his temples with his thumb and index finger. "They'll come."

"Nobody's coming," Brody said.

Ames sat up to look at him, and squeezed his gun close to his stomach. "Ain't no peace, Brody. Ain't no peace no more."

"It's okay," Brody said.

Turning back to stare at the lantern on the ground, Ames wrung his hands around the musket's stock over and over. "Can't come in. Can't breathe in der. Too close, too tight."

Brody waited for several minutes, but Ames seemed to slip away, into a memory of his past.

"I'm sorry, Ames. I wish I could make everything better." Feeling there was nothing else he could do, Brody went back to the house.

The next morning was warm and humid. Brody could barely see the road for the thick mist obscuring it and the treeline that edged the road past the house. He stood on the porch, waiting for Ames to come out of the tent.

Mary stepped into the doorway behind him. "Breakfast is ready."

"Yes, ma'am."

While Brody was eating, Ames came inside. "Eggs and bacon?"

Brody smiled. "There's plenty left."

Ames ate a big piece of crunchy bacon. He glanced at Brody often. After cleaning the kitchen, Mary took a seat across from them and looked hard at Brody, obviously waiting on him to say something.

"I want you to go with me," he said.

Ames stopped chewing and put his fork down. "Where ya goin'?"

"Fort Smith, like I told you last night," Brody said. "I've missed my folks something awful, and I found out they live on the far side of town, now. I want to see them so bad."

Ames picked up his fork and shoveled a bite of egg into his mouth. "I needs ta stay here."

"Well, I have another reason too. We found a dying man and it looks like an animal got him. Some of our traps have been messed with too. I was hoping you could take a look and tell me what you think."

Mary gasped. "A dead man? Brody, you never told me you found a dead man!"

"I'm sorry, Miss Mary. Joe figures he was killed by a bear, but we can't find any bear sign. Or any other animal he recognizes. He is powerful worried, and I am too, 'specially with his little boy in camp with us."

Ames grinned. "I 'member fightin' a mean ol' bear, once. Seems like I also 'member young Brody here makin' sure dat bear didn't eat ol' Ames, either."

Brody laughed. "Boy, I sure don't want to do that again."

Mary placed her hand on top of Ames' crooked fingers and nodded her head. "You should go. Luke can handle things while you're gone."

Placing his fork on the plate, Ames stared at Brody.

The house was quiet. Birds chirped outside. The dog's claws scratched on the porch as it walked past the door. At the back of the house, Buck pawed at the ground, asking for some more grain.

Ames finally wiped his mouth. "If I go, I can't go into town."

"Yes, sir," Brody said. "Just like old times."

Ames smiled. "Just like old times."

"Except," Brody said, "you have to shave,"

"I have to what?"

———

Ames rode a big mule, keeping it in the woods and off the road. "Get on over here, where folks can't see ya."

While riding down the center of the trail, Brody looked back. He raised his hat, allowing him to see Ames. "Come on out here in the road with me. Nobody's going to recognize you with that clean face of yours."

Mumbling something under his breath, Ames turned the mule and came onto the trail behind Brody. The mule kept straying to the edge of the road, reaching and trying to nibble at the green sprigs brought on by spring. Brody laughed each time Ames struggled to get the stubborn critter back to the middle.

After jerking the reins and getting the mule straightened out, Ames pointed at Brody's back. "Where ya get dat rifle?"

"It's the one you gave me." Brody reached and pulled the Henry up where Ames could see it.

"Ya fixed dat old stock."

"Yes, sir. It's not smooth and fancy but it works good."

"Ya shootin' any good with it?"

"Yep."

"With dat gun?"

Brody nodded.

"See dat rock up on da side, up there?"

Looking up the road, Brody spotted a white rock at the edge of the road. "Yes."

"Shoot it."

"Right now?"

Bringing the mule to a stop, Ames waited. "Let's see what ya got."

After climbing down, Brody got the rifle, opened his pack, and reached inside. Finding the opened box of rifle cartridges, he realized he had left his new box in the camp shed. "I don't have many shots to waste," he said to Ames.

Ames teased him. "Ya can't hit it with one?"

Brody loaded his gun. He gave Ames a smile, aimed, and then shot. White dust puffed from the rock's surface.

Ames grinned. "That's my lil' feller."

The sun was high when they reached the river. As Brody paid for the ferry, a tall cowboy with a fancy looking rifle rode up to cross with them. His shiny gun looked as though it had never been shot. He nodded at the ferryman, looked Brody and Ames over, and then ignored them.

The boat rocked gently as the hired hands pulled it across the flowing water. The cowboy polished the rifle and rubbed oil into the action as they traveled.

When they reached the other bank, the fellow stayed behind, telling the ferryman he would be waiting for a friend. Brody was glad to be leaving him there.

Down the road a ways, Ames halted his mule. "I gots to stop up here."

"Come on, Ames, I don't think anyone will know who you are," Brody said. "We'll go around town, so we don't run into any folks."

Ames shook his head.

Brody pulled on the brim of his floppy hat. "You could wear a big hat like this."

Ames laughed. "I'll stay up on dat hill we camped at last time we was here."

Brody watched Ames for a few seconds. "Is everything good with you and your family? I mean, you haven't even been staying in your own house."

Rubbing his chin, Ames looked away. "Feel like I can't breathe right in der, especially at night. I hears lots of things outside. Dem Yankees always sneaking around."

"Nobody's out there," Brody said. "After the shootin' contest, I'd like for you to come with me to see my parents."

Ames looked sharply at Brody. "What shootin' contest?"

Brody cringed. "Uhm, it's just a little turkey shoot they're going to have at the edge of town. I thought it would be fun to go."

Brody swung down from Buck's back and made a show of checking the horse's hoof. "I think he picked up a stone. He seemed to be favoring this foot. What do you think?"

"I think you is tryin' to pull da wool over my eyes. Ya goin' ta watch, or shoot?"

Brody avoided looking at Ames. "To shoot."

Ames exploded with anger. "Why ya going to da town where dere is lawmen lookin' to lock us up, and bad men lookin' to kill us? I thought we was comin' to see yer folks and track a bear in de woods. Did ya loose yer dadburn common sense off wit dem Injuns!"

Brody gritted his teeth. "For about a year now, I have been hiding or running. I've had to lie to good people, sleep on the ground or in ramshackle sheds in all kinds of weather, had more than my share of ticks and chiggers, and struggled to find my own food. I've had to live not knowing where my folks were or even if they were safe, and I haven't felt much like anything but a coward, lately." He ran out of steam and hung his head. "Ames, I really need to do this."

Ames opened his mouth but then shut it. Finally he said, "Good Lord knows ya done put up with my madness on da mountain many a time. I don't like it none, not one bit, but I'll not stop ya."

Brody heaved a huge sigh of relief. "Thank you, Ames."

"I ain't comin' in ta drag yore hide out of dat jailhouse, either, so ya better not get caught."

Brody grinned. "I won't get caught, I promise."

He led buck over beside a fallen log and hoisted himself from it to Buck's back, listening to Ames grumble under his breath the whole time.

They skirted around town and were nearly to the hill where Ames wanted to wait.

"You spent a lot of time in the woods. I want to take you out there and talk to Joe. He half-joked that it was some old Indian legend, but I didn't like the look in his eye when he said it."

"It a big ol' she-bear," Ames said. "I almost guarantee."

"Oh," Brody grinned, "and I can't wait for you to meet Joe's boy, Todd. Keeping up with him is like trying to herd a litter of wild puppies."

"I'd like dat," Ames said. He pulled his big mule to a stop. "Dis is close enough." Through the thin stand of trees, they looked down in the distance at the buildings on the edge of town.

Brody turned Buck toward them. "I'll be back right after the contest." Ames growled something he couldn't catch, but thought he heard the words 'durn fool' a couple of times.

When he reached town, he came in near the stable where his papa once worked. He saw people everywhere. They crossed the streets and went in and out of the storefronts. He had seen anthills with less action.

Keeping his hat low, he did his best to keep from running over folks, or getting in the way of other riders. His thoughts scared him as he imagined someone pointing and yelling, "It's the boy on the reward poster!"

He tried to keep a lookout for a girl with long dark curls. He thought about convincing Sarah to go with him to the contest but then remembered what she said about the Millers talking to her. If they saw him with Sarah, Brody knew a floppy hat wouldn't fool them.

The stables were in sight when he saw a sign nailed to a post at the side of the street. It announced the shooting contest and had an arrow pointing the way. Shots rang out in the distance, somewhere past the horse barn. He nudged Buck into a trot. The contest had already started.

People were gathered all around one end of a long field. Shots came from the front of the crowd and there was a smattering of applause. A few frilly umbrellas were scattered throughout the groups. Some of the women twirled them as they chatted. People were eating food and watching a line of men at the front.

After a few moments, the men raised their pistols and shot at targets farther afield, which resulted in a few more claps and whistles.

Brody jumped off Buck's back and tied him to a fence post. As he turned, he saw Daniel coming through the crowd.

Brody walked toward him, and purposefully bumped him as they passed each other. "Sorry."

The boy glanced around. "It's all right, mister."

Brody grinned and briefly lifted the brim of his hat.

Daniel's eyes grew wide and he jumped toward Brody, hugging him hard. "Mister Brody!"

"Shhh. Hush, Daniel, I don't want anyone else to notice me."

The little black boy immediately straightened up, and started inspecting his fingernail closely, not looking directly at Brody. "I'm powerful happy to see you, but what you doin' back in Fort Smith? Them Miller's sho' would like to get a hold of you."

Brody turned slightly away from Daniel and pretended to watch a couple of men laying odds on which shooters were going through to the next round. "I had to see my folks, and maybe Sarah, too. Besides, this hat hides my face so well, you didn't even notice me."

The boy raised his finger to his mouth, bit off a hangnail and spit. . "Sho' nuff. Don't you worry, none, no sir. I won't let anyone catch on."

"And call me Flint."

Daniel gave a toothy grin. "Dat's a good name. Hard and tough, just like you."

He put a hand over his brow, like he was searching for someone. "I never got to thank you for the pony, mister Brod- I mean, Mister Flint. Dat pony is the most wonderfulest thing ever give to me. You is the best, Mister Brody. Uh... Mister Flint."

More shots cracked in the background.

"Have I missed the contest?"

"They almost done with the pistols," Daniel said.

"What about rifles?"

"Starts real soon." His mouth dropped open, and he looked at Brody. "You plannin' on shootin'?"

"Yes. Do you know where Sarah is?"

"Hoowee, I can't wait to see ya shoot! Oh, and she up there somewhere. She gonna be tickled to see you." Suddenly, he scrunched up his face. "Maybe."

Glancing through the crowd, Brody noticed the tall cowboy they had seen on the ferry. He was weaving between people, making his way toward the front. In his right hand was the shiny rifle.

"I'll go fetch her," Daniel offered.

"No. Don't get her. Don't tell her I'm here. Is she with someone?"

"Eli," Daniel sounded disgusted. "He a new feller in town and I don't care about him none."

Brody unslung his rifle. "Where do I go to enter the contest?"

"You gonna be shootin' against Eli," Daniel said. "He a good shot."

"Show me the way."

Daniel was off in a flash, twisting and turning his body so he could squeeze between people. Brody rushed to keep up. "Not so fast."

He ran straight into a short man wearing a funny cone-shaped hat. The fellow spoke sharply to him in words Brody could not understand, although he could tell the man was not too happy with him.

"I'm sorry," Brody said.

"You slow down," he said with a heavy accent.

"He a Chinese," Daniel said. "He been workin' on dat railroad. Come on, we better hurry."

After they reached the front, Brody saw a table with two portly men sitting behind it. To the side were two large quilts spread on the ground. Things were strewn across both blankets. On the middle of the table were two meaty hams, wrapped in paper. A sign leaned against them announcing Hoffman's Grocery was sponsoring the contest.

"Sign up over there," Daniel said.

"Thanks, Daniel. Wish me luck."

"Yes, sir. I sho' do."

Brody approached the table, but the man wearing the cowboy hat stepped in front of him. He set his shiny gun down and announced he wanted to enter. A few questions later, and the cowboy picked up his gun and strode over to the quilt on the ground.

Brody stepped up to the table and placed his rifle next to the hams. "I'd like to enter the contest."

One of the men on the other side leaned forward. He was well groomed, in his thirties, and wore thick glasses. He adjusted his spectacles and Brody feared the man was trying to get a better look at his face. His heart skipped a beat.

Chapter Nine

"Y ou sure you want to enter?" the man asked.

Thinking as fast as he could, Brody jutted his bottom jaw to the side and twisted his lips into a puckered wrinkle. "I'd like ta enter," he said with the best hillbilly accent he could muster.

The man glanced at his partner next to him and rolled his eyes as he reached out and pulled the Henry closer. He inspected the stock and showed it to the other man, who shrugged. He then handed it back to Brody. "Don't get your hopes up, son. What's your name?"

"Flint. Flint Smith," Brody said, dragging his words out and putting an extra bit of twang in his voice.

The man wrote the name down on a register. "Hoffman Grocery would like to thank you for entering. We hope you win one of the hams. Please visit our store after the contest for all of your grocery needs. The rifle shooter's blanket is over there."

Turning around, Brody saw Sarah talking to the tall boy, Eli. They laughed about something in their conversation and she poked him on the shoulder. Eli leaned on his gun, a new weapon, a repeater of some sort.

Someone shouted behind Brody. "Attention everyone." A man stood in a chair and announced the winner of the pistol competition.

Applause spread through the crowd. "We are now starting the rifle shoot." The man stepped down.

"I refuse to compete against this," a voice said.

Brody peeked from under his hat. His eyes widened when he saw the cowboy pointing at him. "Me?" Brody asked, forgetting his country accent for a moment.

Cowboy redirected his finger to the Henry rifle. "Is this a joke?" he asked the men at the table. Everyone close turned to look at Brody and the cowboy. "You cannot allow him to shoot with that."

The man with the glasses came around the table. "I believe the gun will shoot fine, sir. I've already taken a look at it."

Cowboy looked to Brody and then at the man. "It is a disgrace to be included with that homemade thing."

The portly man leaned close to the cowboy. His whisper was loud enough for Brody to hear. "I'm sure he will be out in the first round."

Several of the men and women nearby laughed. Brody clinched his teeth and glanced around to see if Sarah or Eli had noticed but they were too interested in each other. Cowboy stomped off, muttering angrily.

The man still sitting behind the table waved to get Brody's attention. "We are getting ready to start. What do you have for the blanket?"

Brody looked at the items on the quilt. He saw a knife, some beef jerky, a new bedroll, a saddlebag, and several other items. He remembered his hillbilly tone. "Tarnation, what is this?"

"You haven't shot in any contest before, have you?" the man asked, raising one eyebrow.

"No, sir. I reckon not."

"I see. To make it more interesting, the sponsors allow participants to put something up as an added bonus. Every contestant places a prize here and the winner gets first choice. You can't enter without putting something down."

Hesitating, Brody tried to think of something he could offer.

"Just put something down so we can get started," the man said irritably. "How about your old hat and that knife?"

"No," Brody said, "not the hat." Reluctantly, he removed his big knife and the sheath Ames had made him. He hesitated. "I guess I could use this."

"That will work," the man said.

Brody held his prized knife a few feet above the quilt. His fingers had a mind of their own and his hand squeezed even though he was telling it to let go. When he finally dropped it, the knife seemed to tumble forever before hitting the blanket.

"Line up and stay in that order," one of the men said.

After joining the others, Brody noticed Sarah had sat in the grass near the front of the crowd. He turned his back to her, hoping she would not recognize him.

"First round. Get ready. Farthest from the center is out. If more than one of you miss your board, you are both out."

Brody followed Cowboy to the front, and saw Eli waiting for the other shooters. Logs marked off the shooting area. A few men lay down and propped their guns across the log in front of them. Cowboy stepped forward and snorted. "Twenty five steps."

"Prepare to fire," the official said.

Shaking his head, Cowboy huffed. "I can't believe I rode thirty miles for this joke of a contest."

Each shooter had a target, a wooden shingle, propped against a stump. Each board had a white X across it's middle. At a signal from the man that registered Brody, the contestants took turns firing. Sarah's friend, Eli, who was on the other side of Cowboy, shot his board. He turned toward Sarah and winked. Brody felt his blood boil.

It was Cowboy's turn, and he did not bother to shoulder his rifle. Instead, he shot from the hip. A hole appeared near the center of his target. He looked bored, ignoring the applause from the crowd.

It was Brody's turn. He raised his gun. Someone snickered behind him and another person chuckled. Muffled voices came from the crowd and then more people laughed at him and his strange weapon.

Cowboy laughed the loudest. "You call that ugly thing a gun?"

Brody wanted to prop on the log, but he knew Cowboy would ridicule him even more. Deciding to stand, he brought the carved, oak rifle stock to his shoulder.

"I ain't never seen such a rifle," someone said.

"I'll be surprised if he even hits the board," Cowboy added to the crowd. "If he misses it, good riddance."

The jeering caused Brody to rush his shot. He yanked the trigger and a thumb-sized chunk of wood flew off the edge of the shingle. He had hoped to hit the piece of wood dead center but it simply sat there with an ugly jagged hole.

Cowboy hee-hawed and slapped his thigh. "He almost missed at twenty five steps."

Brody raised his hat enough for the man to see his face and glared at him. Out of the corner of his eye, he noticed Sarah was staring at him, an unpleasant look on her pretty face. Her tight jaw told Brody she had figured out who he was. He ducked his head back down and stepped to the side.

The last man in the row had apparently been celebrating the festivities. He was using a long musket, and the barrel weaved through the air as he tried to aim. Two Indians, wearing black hats, dove for cover when the gun wavered in their direction. The man shot and totally missed the target and the Indians.

A guy hollered, "Get Charlie outta here before he kills someone." Many voices went up in agreement, and two burly men took his gun and hustled the protesting man from the contest. Relieved laughter followed.

"You're out, sir," the contest sponsor at the table yelled after him.

The Indians rolled the stumps to fifty steps and propped new targets against them. During the next round, Brody's nerves settled a bit. Cowboy got the folks laughing again about the 'hillbilly and his gun,' but he paid him no mind. Brody focused on the target and rested his rifle on top of the log.

He fired and hit the board. His bullet was an inch low. The laughing stopped immediately, and a few folks clapped.

Brody had made a good shot, but another man was not so lucky. He was out, leaving eighteen contestants.

The third round had the target staying at fifty steps, making Brody feel confident. Eli hit his target in the center of the white X. Cowboy did the same without hesitation. When it was Brody's turn, he slowed down and took his time. Taking a deep breath, he prepared to fire.

"Boy, your leaving after this shot," Cowboy said.

"Especially after he used up all his luck in the last round," Eli added.

Brody wanted to say something back, but he resisted. After adjusting his rear sight, he breathed slowly and waited until his aim was centered. Squeezing the trigger, the gun kicked and a hole appeared right in the middle of the target.

"Good shot," the official said, taking his glasses off to polished them on his vest.

"Just more luck," Eli said scornfully.

The next shooter looked over at Brody. "How do you manage to hit anything with that ugly gun?"

Brody stood. "I pull the trigger, the bullet comes out and hits the target. Ain't nothing ugly about that."

The man shot and struck his shingle to the right of the X. He glared at his gun. The next two shooters missed their boards entirely. After a few more rounds, the number of shooters was at thirteen.

"Move them," the announcer ordered.

The two Indians came out, rolled the stumps again, and set up new targets.

"Gentlemen, you are now shooting from sixty steps."

Someone tugged on Brody's shirtsleeve. "What are you doing here?"

Turning around, he saw Sarah. Her mouth was curved downward in a tight frown.

Brody kept his head low. "We shouldn't be seen together," he whispered.

Sarah crossed her arms and lowered her voice, "You shouldn't be here at all."

The pressure of the contest and his jealously of Eli pushed Brody over the edge. "And you shouldn't be here with him."

Placing her hands on her hips, Sarah took a step back. "I can be anywhere with anybody I want." She turned on her heel, and went back to the spot at the front of the crowd. Brody saw Eli looking at him with obvious curiosity.

Eli waved goodbye to the first shooter. His prediction was accurate. The man missed the shingle, and it started a string of bad luck for several more contestants. Eli shot and hit a little high. The crowd clapped. On Cowboy's turn, he took a little longer aiming than normal but hit near the center. He pointed at Brody. "You're out for sure."

"Not yet." Brody sat on the ground and got ready. Losing the contest and his hunting knife in front of Sarah wasn't going to happen. Remembering where his previous bullet hit, Brody adjusted the sight higher. He fired and hit the center of the X. The shingle split in half and each half fell to the side. The crowd went wild with applause.

"I don't believe it." Cowboy threw his hands into the air and yelled. "I don't believe it one bit. He shouldn't have even been allowed to enter with that thing."

The next round took the targets out to sixty-five steps. Brody concentrated on blocking out the noise of all the people, fired, and hit the target an inch high. It was the hardest shot he had ever made. One shooter clipped the top edge of his target and a few contestants didn't hit their boards. At the end of the round, Brody, Eli, and Cowboy were the only men left.

The portly announcer stepped to the front and shushed the crowd. "Three shooters left. Hoffman's Grocery would like to wish each of them good luck. Be sure to visit the store after the contest. We will now move the targets for the last time. Seventy steps." The crowd clapped and cheered.

For the first time, a look of dread came over Cowboy's face. Knowing the man was rattled, gave Brody a surge of confidence. He was going to win this contest.

Brody turned to make sure Sarah was watching him, but she was looking at the winner of the previous contest. He and the portly man from the table were standing next to the pistol shooter's quilt. The winner was holding one of the sponsor's hams and the new bedroll.

"Sirs, hold very still," a photographer said. "Oh, and please take off your hat," he said to the winner, "it's casting a shadow on your face." The man juggled his ham and bedroll but managed to get the hat from his head. The photographer took the cap off of the wooden box and looked at his pocket watch. A few seconds later, he replaced the cap and nodded. "Thank you, sirs."

They shook hands all around. "Your picture will be in the front window of Hoffman's Grocery on Main Street," the stout man said. "Come by and bring your friends to see it."

Brody almost dropped his gun. If he won, they would make him take his hat off and his picture would be in a store window on the busiest street in town!

The roar of a rifle jerked Brody out of his panic.

Cowboy stormed through the crowd. "Get out of my way." A few quiet guffaws sounded among the spectators.

"It's just me and you." Eli made a motion for Brody to go first, but he shook his head. He waited quietly while Eli got ready for his shot. He was still for a long while. He fired and the board moved. People cheered loudly. Sarah jumped up and down. Eli walked past Brody. "It's been fun, but hurry and get it over with so I can collect my prizes."

Brody rested his gun across the log, and started to line his sights up. He paused. He stared at his gun and tried to think of the best thing to do. Missing the board would put him out and he would lose. He would also look foolish in front of Sarah. Winning could get him arrested, or worse.

The official chuckled quietly behind him. "I never expected you to be one of the last shooters. I'm impressed, but you need to take your shot. Good luck."

Eli was smiling at Sarah, again. Brody decided to shoot true and not miss on purpose. He would at least try his best in front of Sarah. He decided that if he won, he could grab his knife off the quilt and slip away as the crowd broke up to leave.

All of the distractions had caused him to forget the distance they were shooting. He thought it was at seventy steps, but he wasn't sure. It might as well have been a mile.

He placed his front sight on the X, and only the outside edges of the shingle could be seen. There was hardly any wind, so Brody didn't adjust for a breeze. He moved the rear sight up a tiny bit and then fired. The shingle fell over.

The crowd came alive. People shouted and whistled. The round of applause was loud. Brody couldn't hide his smile. Some of the very people who were making fun of him earlier were now clapping for him.

The Indians grabbed the targets and ran to the front line, handing them over to the official. Brody and Eli waited to see who would be the winner. The official motioned his partner over. They talked with each other, holding the shingles up side by side.

After a few minutes, they brought the targets over and held them up for the crowd to see. "It's too close to call," the announcer said. "They will shoot again!"

The people in the crowd roared with excitement. A few men stepped forward for a closer look at the targets.

"I can do it again," Eli said, as he got ready to shoot. He put a round in the chamber of his rifle.

"What kind of Winchester is that?" Brody asked.

"A new one," Eli replied. "Leave me alone. Stop trying to distract me."

As Eli aimed his rifle, the crowd became silent. Brody looked back to see Sarah watching with both of her fists raised to her mouth. She caught him looking and turned her head away.

He glanced at the photographer. He was turning the box on the tripod to face the rifle winner's blanket, and a man with a badge on his chest was making small talk with him.

"Oh, no," Brody groaned.

Eli's shot rang out and a second later some of the spectators gasped with surprise. The board appeared to be untouched. An Indian came running in from the side and stopped at the target. He held it up and pointed to the top edge.

"It's a hit, but barely," the official announced. Folks cheered, and Eli nodded, doffed his hat, and bowed.

Brody hesitated before taking his turn. All he had to do was make a better shot.

The lawman was now watching them. Brody remembered his promise to Ames that he would not get caught, but losing would be awful. Eli cleared his throat and Brody looked back at him.

The space between Eli's eyebrows was wrinkled with confusion. "What are you doing? It's your turn."

Brody propped against the log, and pointed the Henry at the tiny dot of wood. The wind was still dead. He could aim exactly the same as he had before and win. Gritting his teeth together, Brody brought the gun to his shoulder. The gun barrel warmed the palm of his left hand. Nestling his cheek against the roughly whittled stock, he aimed just to the left side of the target.

"You can do it!" someone yelled.

Brody waited while the shouts of encouragement continued. Out of the corner of his eye, he noticed Eli walk back to the crowd. Brody raised his head, and saw him talk with Sarah for a moment and point at Brody. She shook her head and shrugged.

Brody went back to his aim. It was time for this to be over. He would lose and try to get away as quietly as possible. He fired and immediately got to his feet. A collective groan of disappointment went up from the folk, followed by a burst of applause.

Eli turned to Brody. "I know who you are."

Brody's blood ran cold.

Chapter Ten

One of the Indians looked at Brody's target and waved his arms. The official stepped onto a chair. "It is a miss. Congratulations to our winner." He stepped down and shook Eli's hand. The crowd surged forward to congratulate and clap him on the back, momentarily blocking Eli from view.

Brody was desperately looking for Sarah, when Eli reappeared in front of him with a scowl on his face. "I know what you did." He pointed angrily toward the target. "I know what you did."

The man with the eyeglasses tapped Eli on the shoulder. "Come and pick your item from the quilt. You get first pick and you also win the grand prize." He turned to Brody, "You get second pick. I still can't believe you hung in there till the very end."

All of the shooters gathered around the blanket between Eli and Brody. Brody stayed back, looking for the man with the badge, and to see what Eli would do.

He finally spotted the lawman, preoccupied with talking to a group of women. Brody went to the quilt and sighed with relief. At least he would get his knife back.

"Make your pick," the man from the table said to Eli.

Bending over, Eli reached for the saddlebag. Before his fingers wrapped around the leather, he stopped and looked at Brody. "What did he bring?"

Brody's heart fluttered.

"He brought that big knife."

Brody's heart sank as a wicked grin spread across Eli's face. The boy reached over and drew the knife from the quilt, never taking his eyes off Brody.

"Come get your picture taken," the photographer said to Eli.

Brody turned away and quickly headed into the crowd.

"You haven't picked," someone called behind him.

Brody carefully worked his way through the people, terrified. Trouble had found him again. Eli knew who he was, and he liked Sarah and hated Brody. He expected Eli to start yelling out his real name any second so he could collect the bounty when the lawman swooped in to arrest him.

People slapped Brody on the back as he passed and told him what a nice shot he was. He kept his head low and mumbled his thanks. Buck was waiting patiently where he had been left. Brody quickly untied him, climbed up the fence and slipped onto his back.

The day had not played out the way he had imagined, not at all.

Upon reaching the old camping spot, Brody saw Ames run behind a big pine tree.

Brody stopped Buck and waited but Ames did not come out. "It's me, Ames. What are you doing?"

Slowly, Ames eased his head out to the side of the pine. "Hey, lil' feller. I knowed it was you."

"We need to get going."

Ames limped over and untied the mule. "How good a shootin' ya do?"

Brody slumped and brushed some loose hair from Buck's neck. "I made it to the end, but I missed the last shot."

"How's dat?"

"I lost the contest and my knife, Ames. I didn't do so good."

Ames raised one of his eyebrows. "Dat big ol' sticker I stuck dat bear with?"

"That's the one," Brody eyes watered. "It's gone."

Hoof beats drummed across the field below them. Ames disappeared behind the large pine again and moments later, Tater thundered over the hill with Daniel bouncing all over his back.

Daniel's voice cut in and out with each of the pony's jarring strides. "Mister Brody," he hollered, "I needin' to speak with you."

Before Tater even came to a stop, Daniel jumped down. He rushed over and tugged at Brody's pant leg. "You were shootin' sooo fine. Finest shootin' I ain't never seen."

"Ames," Brody called. "Come on out."

Daniel pointed to the Henry slung across Brody's back. "I think it look fine, just fine."

He thumped Brody on the leg, "Hey, now, that scoundrel, Eli, is wanting to see you. Says he wants to shoot again, just you and him."

"He wants to what?"

"He say come down by the river. Win or lose, you can have dat big knife."

Brody leaned forward. "My knife?"

"Suppose so, and when it's over, I wants you to meet my folks. Dey wants ta see you something awful."

"Hold it, right there," Ames growled, as he stepped from behind the tree, pointing his musket toward them. "Is ye Union or Confederate?"

Daniel threw his hands up high in the air and yelled, "Oh, mercy, sir! Don't shoot, I just da messenger for Mister Flint." He lowered his voice, "Quick, Mister Brody, whip your horse up and run away!"

Brody panicked. "Ames, put that gun up! This is my friend, Daniel."

Ames rushed over. "Brody, someone were following ya."

"It was Daniel," Brody explained. "Nobody else. Right, Daniel?"

Daniel still had his hands up, "No, sir, just me. I be extra careful to keep my friend safe."

Ames lowered his gun and looked Daniel over. "You'll do. Put yer hands down."

"Daniel is a mighty good friend, Ames." He couldn't believe Daniel had risked getting shot to give him a chance to flee.

Daniel stood straighter and smiled. "Dat's right. Me and Mister Brody is good friends. I took dem books to Judge Parker, just like he ask me. Snuck in and put 'em under his big ol' brown desk."

"You did good," Brody said.

"Pa say Billy's world done blowed up. He in a heap of trouble with black folk cause of dem books."

"Your pa said that?" Brody asked.

"Yep, and he say thank ya for givin' Tater to me. He get me ta work and home real fast."

Brody nodded. He looked at Ames. "I have to go down to the river. I think I can get my knife back."

Ames climbed onto the mule's back. "We needs ta get on da road. Ain't no need ta be messin' around here. Da longer we is here the quicker dey gon catch us."

"I need my knife," Brody said. "You don't have to go. Wait up here for me."

"I say it ain't worth it!"

Brody scowled back at Ames. "I am not leaving without my knife!"

They stared at each other for a long moment.

Mumbling under his breath, Ames kicked his mule to come up next to Buck. "Gonna get us both caught."

The agile little boy hoisted himself up onto Tater. Daniel was certainly taking good care of him. His old pony had a glossy coat and a spring in his step.

Daniel pushed Tater in between Buck and the mule. "How long you leavin' for? Will you be back for the hangin'?"

Ames adjusted the reins. "What hangin'?"

Brody and Ames followed as Daniel led the way. The boy's mouth rattled constantly. "Everybody's comin' in September. Five folks is gettin' hung, two of 'em brothers."

"Brothers?" Brody asked.

"Yep, dem Manley brothers kilt a family a while back. Kilt 'em with an axe."

Brody glanced at Ames. "With an axe?"

"Sure did," Daniel said. "One of the farm hands got away after dey chopped his hand off. He told who did it and dey got caught."

Ames snickered, "Well, wit one hand, he shore nuff is a 'farm hand'."

When they arrived at the river, Brody could see two people and a horse. Brody's heart leaped when he saw it was Sarah waiting with Eli.

The spot Eli had chosen was on an inside bend in the river. The area was open and grassy. Behind them, the water rolled quietly.

As they rode up, Daniel said, "Here he is, Miss Sarah. I done bring him like I told you."

Eli interrupted and pointed at Ames, "Who's your friend?"

Ames' lowered his eyebrows and jutted out his jaw. Brody said hastily, "It doesn't matter. Daniel said you wanted to shoot again."

Sarah was standing with her hands on her hips. After nodding at Ames, she looked from Eli to Brody with narrowed eyes. "This is ridiculous."

"We're going to find out who's really the best shot," Eli said.

Brody wanted to laugh. "You didn't tell anybody about me, did you?"

Eli let out a sarcastic chuckle. "That you're really Brody Martin, or that you lost the contest on purpose?"

Ames bellowed, "He knowed who ya are!"

Brody launched himself off of Buck and across Tater's back, knocking Daniel out of the saddle. He was wrestling with Ames to keep him from raising the musket, when he saw Eli snap up his Winchester. Sarah slapped Eli's gun down.

"That's enough!" Brody shouted. "Ames, you're going to end up shooting me. Stop it!"

Ames was breathing heavy, but he quit struggling to get his gun up. "I wouldn't ne'er do such a thing. You knowed I wouldn't."

Brody slowly let go of Ames' musket. "Everything is going to be alright. I'll explain it all later."

He climbed off Tater, and helped Daniel up. "Are you okay?"

Daniel was staring at Brody. "Did you really lose that shootin' contest on purpose?"

Brody walked over to Eli. "Just let me buy my knife back. You won the contest. We don't need to shoot anymore."

Sarah asked, "Why did you take the chance of getting caught, just to enter a contest?"

He wanted to tell her the truth. He wanted to explain that she was the main reason he had chanced a trip into town, but not in front of Eli. "I thought I could win."

Sarah looked disappointed.

"That's enough talk," Eli sneered. "We've got some shooting to do. This is between me and Brody. We don't need a bunch of lookers."

"But I want ta watch," Daniel said.

"No."

"Now, wait a minute," Brody argued. "They can stay if they want."

Eli pulled a hunting knife in a sheath from his horse's pack. Brody recognized it. The sheath was the one Ames had given him, and he recognized the knife handle sticking out of it.

Eli turned, faced the river, and raised his arm over his head as if to throw it in the water.

Brody started toward him. "Wait!"

Eli spun around to face him. "Everybody leaves. There's no reason for them to see you lose again."

"You sure your not afraid you'll be the one losing?" Brody shot back.

Eli pretended to toss the knife in the river again.

"Alright," Brody said, "everybody, go."

Daniel got on Tater, and helped Sarah up behind him. She looked to Eli and Brody, and shook her head. "Let's go Daniel, and let these *boys* play their little shooting game." Daniel looked mighty sad to be leaving, but he turned Tater back toward town.

Ames sidled the mule so close, Eli had to step back. "How come ya don't want no one watchin'? Ya gonna cheat?"

Eli's face turned red and angry, "You better watch it, old man."

Brody stepped between them. "Ames, wait for me back around the bend."

He unslung his Henry, and gave Eli a threatening stare. "There won't be any cheating… right Eli? He just wants a fair shooting match. Then I'll have my knife, Ames, win or lose."

Eli matched his stare. "That's it. I prove I'm the best. You get your knife back. Fair and square."

As Ames rode away, Eli went to his saddlebag and removed a tiny brown pill bottle. He took it and the knife and walked away from the river. When they reached a dirt bank about a hundred steps across the sand, Eli jabbed Brody's knife into the ground and carefully positioned the small bottle on the end of the handle.

Eli headed back to the horses. "First one to hit the bottle wins."

"No, we could hit the handle and ruin it."

"Then you better be careful and shoot straight," Eli said. He got his gun, unloaded it, and then held his hand out for Brody to see. "Only three shots, that's it." He nodded toward the Henry. "How many do you have in there?"

"I don't have many, maybe seven or eight," Brody said.

Eli held his bullets up and then started loading his gun. "Only three. Fair and square, remember."

Brody ejected the remaining cartridges from his rifle. Each one tumbled through the air and landed close to him. He picked them up, twisted the magazine tube open, and dropped three back into the gun.

"Put the rest in your saddlebag," Eli ordered.

While shoving the remaining bullets in his pocket, Brody smiled at him. "You have a lot of trouble counting to three, do you?"

Eli's jaw muscles bulged as he clenched his teeth. "I go first."

Brody looked toward the target while Eli propped his gun across a stump. The dark handle on the knife could be seen but the bottle was nothing more than a brown speck. The tiny target would be almost impossible to hit. "You better not shoot the handle off my knife."

Eli fired and dirt flew up at the side of the target. "Your turn."

Resting his gun on top of the stump, Brody got ready. His front sight covered the knife and bottle completely. "We can't hit that. There's no way."

"I can," Eli said.

"Well, you didn't." Brody aimed high, hoping not to destroy his knife. He shot and saw the impact on the dirt bank behind the target.

"Just warming up, is all." Eli took his turn and missed. This time, his bullet hit just in front of the handle.

"I don't want to do this anymore, that knife is a good one, and one of us is going to mess it up," Brody said. "Let me buy it back from you."

"Nope. You don't shoot, it's my knife." Eli shook his head. "And since I already have a knife, I'll probably just toss that one in the river."

Brody was shocked. "You'd really do that? The knife was handed down from my papa, and it means a lot to me."

"Then you shouldn't have put it on the blanket," Eli said.

Brody took a deep breath, figuring Eli was just trying to rattle him so he would miss. He aimed with a full bead, keeping the top of his front sight even with the top of his back one. Squeezing the trigger slowly, the gun jerked against his shoulder. He looked toward the brown bottle but couldn't see it. "I think I hit it."

"You didn't hit it," Eli argued.

Brody stood up and peered at his knife. "I don't see it."

"Well, go take a look," Eli said, "but you didn't hit it."

Brody headed toward the dirt bank. As he neared the target, he noticed the glass container had been shattered into dozens of tiny pieces. He had hit the bottle, which meant the knife was his. It was all he could do to keep from jumping up and down. "I hit it. Come and look."

A stick snapped at the top of the dirt bank. Two men jumped out of the brush, with guns drawn. Brody panicked as he recognized Billy and Frank Miller. Without saying a word, Frank raised a pistol and shot, but Brody was already sprinting toward his horse.

Billy shouted, "Time to pay, troublemaker!"

Chapter Eleven

Two more blasts came from behind Brody. Eli was already scrambling over a stack of river logs, and Brody headed for them. He stumbled and fell. On his way down, he rolled behind the stump he and Eli had been using as a prop.

He peered around it and saw that Billy had fallen at the bottom of the steep bank. Frank was helping his father up with one hand and aiming the pistol toward Brody with the other.

There was only one round left in the Henry. Brody reached in his pocket to grab some more cartridges but Frank fired. Bark splintered off the top of the stump and hit Brody's hat. He ducked and lay down next to it, aiming the rifle toward the men.

Billy was back on his feet. "Come here, you little coward!"

Brody stole another glance around. Both of the ambushers were headed his way. He only had one quick shot. They would be on top of him before he could reload.

Brody aimed at Billy's cowboy boots and fired. Billy faltered at his next step and went to the ground, grabbing at his foot and shouting obscenities. Frank stopped running and yanked on Billy's arm, trying to get him on his feet again. It was the break Brody needed.

He jumped to his feet and dashed to Buck's side. Pure fright sent him scampering up onto the horse's back. Grabbing the reins with one hand, he slung his rifle over his shoulder and kicked Buck's sides. Sand flew up from his hooves as he dug in, and they raced toward the bend. Brody saw Eli picking his way back over the logs.

"Run!" Brody shouted. "They'll shoot you, too!"

He kicked Buck again, and the horse doubled his speed as they reached firmer ground. Another shot came but Brody didn't look to see if it was from Billy or Frank. Limbs slapped at his face and arms as they raced between the trees. He had escaped with his life, but without his knife.

Just as Brody reached a trail, he met Ames and his mule lumbering toward them. He jerked on the reins and Buck slid to a stop.

"What's goin' on? You all right?" Ames asked. "I heard a bunch of shootin'. Sounded like pistols."

Brody took several deep breaths. "It's the Millers. We've got to get out of here."

They rode hard, down to the main road. Ames turned his mule and headed into the woods. Brody followed and they stopped at the top of a ridge. Buck and the mule huffed for air.

They let their mounts cool and then rode down the side of the ridge. "As soon as we cross the ferry, we'll stay off the road," he said to Ames.

"What happen back there?"

Brody explained how the Millers had snuck up on them while they were shooting and that even though he had won, he still lost his knife.

Ames sighed loudly, making a whistling sound. "We gotta stay out of Fort Smith fer sure. Don't reckon yer gonna get to see your folks."

"I guess they wouldn't be safe if the Millers thought I was back with them anyway." Brody stared between the ears of his horse, missing his parents so much that his eyes burned and he had to bite his lip.

He finally broke the silence, "I shot Billy."

"Kilt him?"

"No. I shot him in the foot."

"Shot him in da foot?"

"Yes, in the foot."

Ames chuckled. "Thought you was a good shot."

They rode for a few more minutes before Brody spoke again. "I could've killed him." He cleared his throat. "I just couldn't."

"You done right, lil' feller," Ames said. "You done right."

After taking the ferry, they continued for another hour, stopping every once in a while to listen. When the sun dipped below the horizon, Brody pulled back on the reins. "I promised Joe I'd be back this evening, but it's getting dark and we still have miles to go."

"We gonna have ta camp," Ames said. He walked his mule down to a little rocky creek. Brody followed. A huge cliff rose up on one side, and slabs of stone angled up from the ground on the other to form a deep ravine. There was a small open area between two large broken boulders. "Dis here will work fine."

Taking his hat off, Brody rubbed a hand through his hair. "I'm worn plumb out." He slapped at a mosquito. "Darn bugs are already out."

Ames got off the mule and limped over. "My hind end is aching." He rubbed his knee. "My leg too."

Brody slid off Buck and opened his saddlebag. He dug around until he found his matches and pulled three out. "You'll like Joe and

Todd." He saw the apples that were left in his bag and held one up. "You want an apple?"

"Ye bet cha'. They go right nice wit dis. " Ames brought out some cornbread and dried meat that Mary sent.

Breaking sticks in half, Brody made a small pile of wood. "Joe is taking me to see his marshal friend tomorrow evening."

"You sure dat what ye need ta do?"

Brody struck one of the matches and quickly held it under the twigs. Fire flamed up on the first try. He put the other two in his pocket. "I'm tired of all this. The Millers tried to kill me today. They're not going to stop. Joe says if I tell this marshal everything, he can get it all straightened out, but it's got me worried."

He blew gently on the flames. "They could just throw me straight in jail. I think I'm going to see my folks first. I can't hardly wait for that."

Ames tilted his head and seemed to be thinking hard about something. "Wish I could meet yer folks," he finally said. "But I just can't risk gettin' catched. We gots ta get dem crops planted."

"I don't expect you to go, Ames. I'll talk to the marshal. You don't even have to come back to Fort Smith with me."

"It don't feel right, lettin' ye go back all by yerself.

"I won't be alone. Joe is coming and I'm sure Papa will, too." Brody could see Ames was still uneasy about the situation. He scooted back against one of the boulders.

"We're going to take up all the traps in the morning. Joe thinks a bear took off with one of them, and it even tore out some saplings, roots and all. I'd like for you to look at it. Joe says it's probably the same thing that killed that man."

"I can do dat," Ames said. "Tell me bout dat dead feller y'all found."

Brody shivered, and not just because it was getting chilly. "He had strange cuts, in pairs, close together like the animal only had two claws. It was weird and creepy."

Ames shook all over, as if he had the willies. "Brody, dat sound like a pure de old wampus cat. Ye don't needs ta be messin' around there anymore."

"What's a wampus cat?"

Standing, Ames held a hand out and raised it to shoulder height. "About dis tall, yellow eyes, and evil. You remember dat Red Eyes we seen back on yer farm?"

"Yes. People have seen Red Eyes all over where I grew up."

"A mean ol' wampus can eat two of dem Red Eyes of yourn. We don't need ta be goin' in dat place."

Brody watched Ames for a moment. "Joe thinks it's some Indian legend and you say it's some kind of giant cat. I think it might be a bear." Brody wasn't totally convinced it was a bear but he could see fear in his friend's face.

"I'd like ta meet yer friends and all, but ol' Ames can't spend another night away from home."

"It's not a wampus cat," Brody said, "and we won't spend the night. We'll be gone long before dark."

"You sure bout dat?"

"Joe will be up at daybreak, pulling traps. He'll probably have it all done by the time we get there. You and I can take a look around and help them pack. Then, we can leave."

"I jes' don't know," Ames said.

"Listen, Ames. What if it is something bad? We need to know. Joe and his little boy will be back out there next year, trapping. They need to know what it is and you're the one who can tell us."

"Me?"

"You lived on the Devil's Backbone for years. I don't know anybody who's survived off the land longer than you. You're a great tracker, trap setter, and hunter. I may be trapping out there next year too. You want me camping out there, not knowing what's in the woods?"

Ames flapped his hands at Brody. "Fine. I'll go and tell ye what it is. Then we leavin', right?"

"Yes, sir."

"Before dark?" Ames asked.

"Yes, sir. Before dark." Brody lay down on his horse blanket. "I have a question."

"What are it?"

"When did you find out you were going to be a grandfather?"

Ames smiled. "I got dat bit of news right after we got to Crawford County."

"I bet you are excited."

"Oh, yes."

"What are you going to do when you have a little baby running around the house?"

Rubbing his hands together, Ames squatted next to the fire. "We gonna picnic."

"Picnic? I think hunting or fishing would be more fun."

Ames sat and stretched his legs out in front of him. "My Ma always talked of goin' on a picnic. She wanted ta take me and Pa so bad but we never got to."

"I remember a picnic with my folks," Brody said. "My grandfather was there, and we had fried chicken and snap peas. I was little but I still remember that day. Being with family and sharing food makes good memories."

Ames took his boots off. "All dis talk of food done made me hungry again. We gonna hafta get some rest before I start eatin' my ol' mule." About that time, the mule in question snorted loudly, making both of them laugh.

They left early the next morning, but Ames refused to stay on the road, prolonging the trip an extra hour. Brody had trouble recognizing the correct turns. Three times, he rode onto the trail in order to get his bearings.

The scent of spring honeysuckle made Brody's stomach growl. The sweet smell always made him want to eat the flowers whole. Sometimes he would pick the blooms and pinch the bottoms. If he pulled the stem out carefully, a tiny drop of delicious nectar would appear. Those carefree days were long gone.

"Hello in the camp," Brody hollered, as they came into sight of it. He expected Todd to come running out of the shed, but he was nowhere to be seen. Everything was quiet. The horses were gone, and there weren't any smoking coals left in the fire pit.

Ames dismounted and stretched his sore muscles. "Dat's a long ride. Where everybody is?"

Brody got down and walked to Joe's wagon. One of the wheels was lying on the ground, along with a hammer and a newly carved spoke. "He's fixing his wheels. Brody went to the shed. "I guess they've gone to pull the traps, but I figured they would be back by now." He reached for the rickety door but froze when he saw a splash of dark red soaked into the ground in front of it.

Jerking the door open, Brody was faced with a twisted mess of blankets, clothes, and other supplies. Everything in the shed had been tumbled. Spots of red were speckled on the floor and some of the bedding. "Ames, get over here."

As soon as Ames was at his side, Brody pointed at the wet ground. "There's blood here, and inside."

Ames pulled Brody back, and stuck his head in the shed. "Whew, what a mess." He crouched down and rubbed his finger across a red spot. "It done dried on top, but still wet on da bottom. I'd say dis here is from yestiday late, or way early dis mornin'."

Brody felt the hairs come up on his arm. He faced the woods and put his hands around his mouth, letting loose with a loud call. Ames came outside. "Why you makin' dat noise."

"Shhh… I need to listen." A breeze rustled the leaves, Buck stomped his foot, and they could hear birds farther out from camp. Brody tried again. "Ehwhooooo!"

Ames cupped a hand around one ear and turned his head from side to side.

Brody called again and again.

Ames finally shook his head. "Ain't nobody answerin' ye." He rubbed his chin and then slowly knelt to the ground, wincing when his knee popped loudly. Bending low, he said, "Smell dat copper. It's a powerful lot o' blood, Brody."

"What happened?" His throat was so shriveled with fear for Joseph and Todd that he could barely get the words formed.

Pointing at the ground, Ames said, "See dis here? Dis blood is cast out dis way. Whoever left dis trail is runnin' dat direction." He nodded toward the east, behind camp.

Brody faced east and cupped his hand around his mouth. "Joe!" His voice was quickly absorbed by the thick trees.

Ames got on all fours and leaned close to the ground around the bloodied earth. "Dat's a big track headed dat way, but a little track going de other way."

"It's Todd. What happened here, Ames?"

Ames reached out for Brody's hand, and groaned a bit when he pulled himself up. He looked inside the shed. "Somthin' bad."

Brody started to take off in the direction of Todd's tracks.

"Wait," Ames said. "Ain't no use takin' off till we figure it out."

"They've been attacked," Brody said. "They're hurt and we need to find them."

Ames placed his palm on Brody's shoulder and squeezed gently. "We gonna look it over first. Might be dat big ol' cat I was tellin' about."

"They isn't no such thing," Brody said forcefully.

"We gonna look it over," Ames said. "Ye go runnin' off and might be going in da wrong direction."

Brody paused and realized he was breathing hard. He took a deep breath and nodded at Ames.

Ames went inside and stood in the middle of the shed. Brody followed but stopped at the doorway. Ames studied the floor, each of the walls, and everything in the room. "On de door," he said, pointing toward Brody.

Brody looked at the inside of the door. Two faint, long scratches ran across it diagonally. "No, Ames. No. It's the same thing that killed that man." His stomach turned and he felt sick. He ran outside and bent over, trying not to heave.

Ames came out and studied the faint tracks on the packed earth. "De big feller went east fer sure. He bleedin' pretty bad."

Coming over and leaning down, Brody looked at the tracks. A smaller shoe print faced west. "Why are they going in opposite directions?"

"See dis big print here?" Ames drew a circle around a large smudge in the dirt. "I don't know what dis is, but it's following yer friend. He were leadin' it away from da boy."

"Is that an animal track?" Brody asked.

"Don't know," Ames answered. "It weren't no cat, and I don't know what it were but it ain't no animal I ever seen."

"Can you find Joe?"

"I reckon I can. He left a good trail."

Brody unslung his gun. "I'm going to look for Todd."

"We needs ta stay together," Ames fussed.

Brody shook his head. "We have to find them before dark. We don't want to still be looking when the sun goes down." He motioned toward the woods. "Hurry, find him and meet me back here."

Ames nodded. "Stay close on da ground. Dem tracks gonna be hard ta see."

Brody ran down the hill, looking frantically in every direction. The tender spring grass had been mashed flat with each of Todd's running steps, but when the trail hit the big woods Brody lost it. There was no more grass, just leaves. He tried to stay patient and look for the next trace of a footprint, but his worries about Todd won over.

Taking a deep breath, he bellowed, "Todd!" Brody ran through the woods, calling out for the boy, until he stumbled over a tree root. He stopped and leaned against a tree.

The sun was sinking lower in the sky. There had been no signs of Todd since entering the big woods. He began to worry he had gone the wrong way, so he forced himself to backtrack to the wood-line.

He found the last place he had tracked Todd. A broken vine, and a gouge in the grass showed where the little boy had fallen hard. Going to his knees, Brody studied the ground. Todd's next step had taken him into the woods.

A few twisted leaves on the forest floor showed where he had turned. Brody missed it earlier in his hurry. He saw a few more disturbed leaves, and a snapped limb. He had Todd's trail again.

Chapter Twelve

An hour later, Brody felt as though he had not gone more than a hundred steps. Crawling on the ground, he took his painful time and when the tracks started up a ridge, he was able to stand again. Todd's boots had slipped on the incline and left an easy path to follow.

After working his way over two more ridges, Brody started to panic again. Long shadows were cast into the woods.

He hung the rifle on his shoulder with its sling, and cupped both hands around his mouth. "Todd!"

Brody took another step but froze when he thought he had heard a faint cry. After waiting for a few moments, he called out for Todd again. This time, he remained motionless and listened. The sound came again, a weak wail from the hollow below.

He dashed down the hill. "Todd, where are you?"

Sliding to a stop at the bottom, Brody waited. A rustling came from a brush pile nearby. "Todd?"

A shape burst from the thick cover and rushed his direction. Brody reached for his gun, but realized it was Todd scrambling toward him. The boy came in so fast and hard that it knocked Brody on his backside. As he hit the ground, Todd was on him, squeezing and gulping great breaths as if all the air had disappeared from the world.

Sitting up, Brody tried to pry him off but the boy refused to let go. "Are you hurt?" Brody asked.

Todd kept his face pressed tightly against Brody's chest. Tears flowed from the corners of his clinched eyelids and he shook hard. Brody struggled to his feet with Todd clinging to him.

"Todd. What happened?"

Todd kept his face buried. Brody reached up to loosen the strangle-hold around his neck.

"Your skin is cold. Let me see if you're hurt." The bone necklace slipped out of Brody's shirt and dangled in the air. Todd grabbed it and squeezed.

He tried to put the terrified boy down, but he wouldn't let go. Brody managed to pry a hand loose. "How long have you been hiding?" Once again, there was no answer. Brody wanted to ask about Joe, but was afraid it would make Todd's reaction even worse. "It's getting dark. Let's get you back to camp."

Todd whimpered. He slid down and clutched Brody's hand hard. Brody tried to lead the boy back up the ridge, but Todd dug his heals in and shook his head violently. He pulled Brody in the direction of the brush pile.

"It's getting dark," Brody said. "We have to go back."

Something crunched in the leaves behind him on the ridge. They froze and watched a large, dark shape stop behind a tree. A rounded hump, covered in brown hair, was sticking out from behind the thick pine. Todd began to cry silently.

Brody's heart hammered. The creature was in the woods with them, less than a hundred steps away.

Brody tried to back up, but Todd was right behind him and he tripped and went to the ground. He came up with the rifle, pointing it toward the thing in the woods. The creature stayed behind the trees.

They were cut off from camp. Brody tried to get a better aim, but the animal faded deeper into the gathering gloom. Hoping to scare it away for good, Brody shouted, "Hey! Git on out of here! Git!"

Pulling Todd to his feet, he swung the boy around to face him.

"Todd, listen to me. We're going to get back to camp. I think I scared it away, so we're going to run like we never have before. I need my hands free to keep my rifle ready, so hang on to my belt and don't let go. Okay?" Todd didn't even blink, he just stared at Brody.

Brody tugged on his hand, and was relieved when Todd followed him without protest. He placed the little boy's fingers on his belt, and Todd hung on to it.

He took long strides, and Todd struggled to keep up. The woods closed in and tugged at their clothes. Yanking away from the undergrowth, Brody pulled him along. Behind them, the loud *ker-hump* of a falling limb spurred them to move even faster. He cast a look over his shoulder and sucked in a breath.

"Run."

Todd looked behind them and collapsed to the forest floor. Brody slid to a stop, and slung the gun across his back. He yanked the boy up into his arms and ran.

The dead weight in his arms made Brody's muscles ache. His legs churned up the hill and down the other side. He looked back, just in time to see a shapeless form crest the top behind him and flow down into the shadows. It was closing the gap between them.

Brody was having trouble seeing the small limbs in the fading light, and they stabbed at his face and eyes as he weaved through the trees along the side of a ridge. Out of the corner of his eye, he saw movement above them. Incredibly, the creature was flanking them.

Coming to a stop, he let Todd slide to the ground. He reached back for his gun and pointed the rifle toward the shifting shadow. He pulled the trigger. The hammer snapped but the gun didn't fire. He had forgotten to reload after the Miller's attack.

He shoved a hand in his pocket and grabbed the cartridges. Five left. His last, new box was still in the shed. His fingers shook so badly, he couldn't force the tube open. A cartridge dropped to the ground.

At last he got the tube open and shoved the shells inside. He jacked a round in the chamber and fired in the creature's direction. In the heat of the moment, he didn't even feel the gun kick.

The massive animal stood on two legs for a moment before hunching over and dropping off the other side of a hill. Brody's mind screamed *bear,* but something was not right. It didn't matter. He had no time to figure it out.

The twilight deepened until he could not see more than fifteen feet in front of him, and he knew full dark would be on them in a matter of minutes.

Brody dug through the leaves, grabbed the fallen shell, and put it in his pocket. He pulled Todd up and started dragging him with one hand.

A huge shape lurched out of the gloom, and Brody fell back clutching Todd close. His gun barrel wavered, and Brody searched for a target, but the thing had vanished just as quickly as it appeared. A horrible odor filled his nostrils. He knew that smell. It was the rank smell of a long dead animal.

"Get away!" Brody yelled. He could hear the creature circle, snapping twigs and limbs as it moved through the gloom. Todd woke up and began to flail. Brody grabbed him around his chest and picked him up with one hand. With his other, he lifted the Henry and fired.

Loud moans came from the darkness, cries that reminded Brody of the time he found a cow caught in a briar patch. Deathly calls and growls filled the air and sent chills across Brody's skin. He yelled into the woods, "Get out of here!"

It slipped into the blackest shadows. A mournful cry pierced the darkening woods.

He put Todd down but held tightly to his hand. "Don't let go," he whispered. Trying to walk as quietly as possible, he changed directions. At first, there was only the sound of their footfalls, and Brody began to think it was gone.

Tiny rustlings to the right soon dashed all hope. He could hear the leaves crunching as it paralleled them. "Stop it." Brody yelled. The animal gurgled in the darkness. Brody fired again and the creepy sound stopped.

Grabbing Todd by the shoulders, Brody shook him. "Run."

This time the boy stayed with him. The woods had flattened out, and the trees were farther apart. The moon was rising, and Brody could see enough to avoid running into tree trunks.

A grunting cough in the woods would spur them on each time they slowed, sometimes sounding right behind them. Each time Brody yelled at it, he could hear it move off. It was playing with them.

Todd stumbled over and over. Brody yanked him up each time and pulled him onward, until Todd fell and wouldn't get up. Straining and pulling, Brody tried to drag him but was too exhausted.

Realizing he couldn't go any farther and wouldn't be able to see this thing coming, Brody grabbed at his shirt pocket. He found some jerky and tossed it down. Deeper in the pocket, he felt what he was looking for, the two extra matches from the night before.

After raking leaves and sticks into a pile, he placed one of the matches against the gun barrel. He pressed the tip to strike it, but it crumbled and broke apart.

The thing in the woods grunted and came closer. Straining to see the animal, Brody pointed the Henry in the direction of the noise and fired. The footfalls moved off and circled around.

With fumbling fingers, Brody tried to strike his last match. He raked it along the barrel but nothing happened. He tried again and again. Running his thumb and finger along the match, he found it was upside down. He flipped it around, struck it against the gun, and it sprang to life. Brody shoved the match against the dead leaves and the fire spread.

Todd sat up. In the flickering light, he stared at the flames with a blank expression, then crawled closer to the growing fire and curled up on the ground.

Brody tossed more wood on the fire. The ring of light spread outward. "Todd, are you all right?"

Todd didn't move.

A gurgling sound came from close by. Shifting quickly, Brody pointed his gun toward the blackness. He was terrified of this creature, but he was desperate to stay alive.

As fast as he could, he grabbed dead limbs and sticks and threw them on the fire. Light was keeping this thing away. Light was keeping them alive. Darkness would bring death.

Knowing he had fired several times, he pulled the Henry's lever down to check the chamber. The gun was empty. Fear coursed through him until he remembered the shell he had dropped. Frantically, he fished the last cartridge out of his pant's pocket. Standing, he shoved his last bullet into the Henry and aimed toward the wall of darkness beyond the firelight. As the fire died back, the light shrank and Brody listened intently.

He couldn't see past the fading firelight, nor did he hear anything else for a while, nothing but the crackling of the flames. He hoped if he hadn't hit it, at least he had scared it away. He breathed a sigh of relief and scrounged for tinder as far into the pressing dark as he dared.

A loud crack startled him. It was still there.

A burning limb crumbled, sending up a shower of sparks before it died away to glowing embers. The ring of light halved in size. He heard soft footfalls just beyond the light.

Brody tossed more limbs on the fire and watched the light quickly grow. He caught movement of a dark shadow. The butt of the gun was on his shoulder in a second, but the monster had already moved deeper into the woods.

He lowered the rifle. There could be no more wild shots. There was only one bullet left.

Little Todd was lying next to the fire. The shocked and exhausted boy was still unconscious, defenseless.

Brody recalled the dying man by the creek. He had been gouged and scored multiple times by this strange two-clawed creature.

He tightened his jaw. As long as he was still alive, he wouldn't let the same thing happen to Todd.

Far across the mountains, the sky lit up. Lightening danced a jagged path across the sky, and moments later deep thunder boomed. Brody waited for the sound to die away. He put the last stick into the precious fire.

Please, please… don't let it rain.

⚓

The wind twisted its way through the treetops, bringing the fresh smell of rain. Moment's later, large drops began to splatter on the ground. Brody leaned over Todd and the fire, trying to shelter them both.

His efforts hardly made a difference. The sky opened up, letting the rain pour freely. Each drop steamed as it hit the embers, and the flames dwindled. Brody stood up. Todd began to whimper softly.

Brody placed one foot on each side of Todd. He held the gun at his hip, ready for the attack. Splattering raindrops stopped him from hearing the creature, but he knew it was there. It would charge through the dark, he would fire his last shot, and then fight to his dying breath.

"When I shoot, it's going to be right on top of us. You need to run," Brody whispered. The boy stopped crying, but he didn't move. "Are you listening, Todd? *You've got to run.*"

"Come on!" Brody shouted into the night. "What are you waiting for?"

There was a lull in the rain. The woods around him began to glow, and a shadow appeared in the woods – his shadow. Twisting around, he saw a lantern bobbing closer.

The light lowered, revealing Ames standing behind it. His rain-slicked face showed his worry, as did his wide eyes. "I like ta never found ye."

It took Brody a few seconds to find his voice. "There's something out here. Something bad."

Ames held the lantern up and steam rose from its top as the rain started up again. He nodded toward the boy. "He alive?"

"He's scared something awful, but I don't think he's hurt. Let's get him out of here." Brody pulled Todd to his feet, but the boy's knees gave way.

"Keep that light up high," he said to Ames. "That thing is close by." Straining with all his might, he tried to pick Todd up but failed. He wiped the rain from his eyes. "I can't do it."

Ames handed Brody the lantern. He bent from his waist and pulled Todd up. Before the boy could sink back down, he grunted and heaved him up over his shoulder. "We gonna go slow, wit my bad leg, but I'll carry the lantern and ye keep yer gun at da ready."

Brody gave the lantern back to Ames and he lifted it high. The rain continued to pelt them, making it hard to see. Brody wiped his face constantly, afraid he wouldn't see the creature until it was too late.

An hour later, they struggled into camp. There had been no sign of the monster, and the rain was finally slacking off. Brody held Todd while Ames limped to his mule. He rubbed his bad knee, placed the lantern on the ground, and winced before climbing up. "Hand him to me," he said. "We ain't camping here."

Brody strained, pushing Todd up into Ames' arms. After Ames had a secure grip, Brody grabbed the lantern and headed for the camp shed.

"Where ye headed?"

"I've got to get my cartridges."

"Ye durn fool. We gots ta get on out of here."

"I've only got one left, Ames. Give me just a second." To his relief, the last box of ammunition was still where he had left it. He grabbed it and sprinted back to the horses. After loading his gun, he got on Buck's back and they left.

Riding Buck at a gentle walk, Brody was overcome with exhaustion. He nodded off several times, his hands wound tight in the horse's mane. Buck stepped into a dip in the road and startled Brody awake. He watched the clouds float away, leaving a clear, bright moon. Turning to Ames, he spoke quietly, "Did you find Joe?"

Ames shook his head. "Dat blood…" He glanced down at Todd. The boy's head rocked with each step the mule took. "Dem spots turned north and down in a holler and ta a creek. He went in da water and I don't think he come out."

Brody had grown close to Joseph. If there were any chance he was still alive, he wanted to go look, and soon. "I found Todd in a brush pile. Maybe Joe was hiding too."

"Dat thing's tracks followed him on down to da creek. It probably catched him right in da water."

"I don't want to believe that," Brody said.

Ames stayed quiet for a while. Pulling back on the reins, he stopped his mule. "We gone fer enough. We can camp here."

"No," Brody argued. "Something's wrong with Todd. We need to get help."

"I seen men act dis way in da war. He gonna be all right. He just seen somethin' awful."

"He isn't a man. He's a boy, a little boy. We're taking him to my momma."

Reaching over, Ames put his hand on Brody's shoulder. "We a long way off and it's dark."

"I don't care," Brody said. "I can't take this anymore. It's just too much." He squeezed the reins. "I've avoided my folks for a long time. I don't want to cause them any trouble, but I can't do this alone anymore."

Ames patted him on the back. "You ain't alone, Brody."

Brody nodded, realizing he might have hurt his friend's feelings. "I'm sorry. I shouldn't have said it that way."

"Let's get going," Ames said. "We got a long ride."

They didn't speak again for hours. No one met them on the road, and they reached the river at daylight and took the first ferry across, giving the horses a much needed rest. On the outskirts of town, Ames wanted to stay hidden by traveling around it. Brody insisted that the fastest way to his folks was through it, and he wasn't going to argue.

The streets were nearly empty. They stayed off of the main road, but there were still storeowners arriving to open the doors for early shoppers. A few glanced at the weary, ragged travelers, but most were too intent on their own business to care.

"Brody, I can't be here."

"Let's hurry," Brody said. "I don't want to be here either. Sarah said my folks moved south of town."

Ames kicked at his mule's sides. "Dis is really somethin'. Can't believe it. I needs ta get out. Fort Smith is going ta get me, Brody."

"We will be all right," Brody said. "We'll be out of town in a few minutes. Sarah said they lived at the edge of a prairie."

They found acres of flat land south of town. Following a muddy, rutted road, they stopped at two places but didn't find anyone home. At the third farm, Brody spotted a boy outside doing his morning chores. He asked him about the Martin house, and the boy gave him directions.

On the east side of the prairie, Brody spotted an old frame house. It looked big enough to have three or four rooms. It was worn but sturdy and recently whitewashed, and though the porch sagged just a bit in the middle, it had two rockers on it, sitting side by side.

A small corral had been recently built to the side and back of the house. A man stood near the pen, pushing hay under the fence with his foot. Two gray mules grabbed mouthfuls of the hay.

Tears began to fill Brody's eyes. "That's my papa." After jumping down from Buck's back, he handed the reins to Ames.

Brody's father looked in their direction. "Be with you in just a minute," he hollered.

He pushed the last of the hay under the fence and walked closer, leaning slightly and holding his side. As he neared the front of the house, he smiled. "Can I help…" his voice trailed off. "Brody? Brody!"

Chapter Thirteen

B rody ran straight into his father's arms, tears falling as fast as the rain had earlier. Papa gathered him in a great bear hug.

Someone crashed into them, almost knocking them over. He felt hands, grabbing and squeezing. Loud sobs were right in his ear and a familiar scent filled the air.

"Momma," he said, turning his head and pulling her closer.

Strong arms hugged him. Soft hands grabbed his face, and his momma pressed her forehead to his. "Oh, my boy, my Brody boy," she murmured over and over.

Brody finally untangled himself from his parents and stepped back to look at them. Papa was leaner, and he was slumped slightly, holding one hand to his side. Momma had more streaks of gray in her hair, but her smile warmed him from the inside out.

His heart overflowed with joy.

A blast of questions came from them both. So many at one time he could not sort them out. He did gather the gist of what they were asking and why. They had been worried sick about him.

"I'm all right," he said over and over.

Momma held his face in her hands and her tone grew more serious. "Where have you been?"

He lowered his head. "I'm sorry Momma. Don't be angry with me."

She wiped her eyes. "I'm not mad."

He looked at her.

She burst into tears and laughter. "I'm just glad to have you back from the dead." She reached out and rubbed the rough skin on Brody's forehead. "What happened to my baby?"

Hugging her again, he noticed how bony she was. "You've lost weight," Brody said.

Pulling them toward the house, Papa said, "We can't stay out here."

Brody was about to follow his father when he heard Todd scream.

"Father!" Todd twisted and squirmed, scratching at Ames' face.

Ames tried to hold him still so he wouldn't fall off the mule. "I can't hold him much longer." Ames grunted.

Brody took his mother's hand and pulled her toward the mule. "He needs help, Momma."

Ames handed Todd down. Momma started crooning to him in a singsong voice, and the boy wrapped his arms around her neck. Soon he was quiet, again, his face buried in her hair. She whispered softly to the child in her arms as she headed toward the house, casting long looks back at Brody.

Ames got down from the mule. "Mister Martin, you mind of I put these critters in wit yer mules?"

"Of course not. Why don't you do that, and then come on up to the house." Papa had a hand on Brody's shoulder as they walked after Momma.

Momma stopped in front of the door. "Who is this Indian boy? And where have you been?"

Brody sighed. He wasn't sure how his folks, especially his mother, was going to take what he had to tell them. He didn't even know where to start.

"His name is Todd. His mother was a half-blood and died when he was four. His father is a Cherokee, Joseph Wolf." He leaned close to his mother's ear and whispered. "Todd saw something terrible. I didn't know how to take care of him, so I brought him to you."

Momma swayed back and forth the whole time they talked. She looked down at the face on her shoulder and pushed a lock of shaggy black hair back. Todd's eyes were closed and he was breathing deeply and evenly. "He's asleep. I should put him in our bed, Jim."

Ames limped up to the porch steps. Brody smiled.

"And this is Ames."

"I've heard about you," Momma said to Ames. "You stay outside."

"Momma." Brody was shocked. "Ames is my friend."

She pointed at a rocking chair. "Have him sit down there until we've had a chance to talk. I'm going to lay this poor boy down." She went inside.

"Ames," Brody said, "I'm sorry. I don't know why Momma would act that way."

"It's all right –," Ames started to say, but Papa interrupted.

"I know why. There's been talk around Fort Smith that he murdered a woman years ago, and more recently, one of the Miller brothers. On top of that, he is also accused of horse thieving."

Ames sat still in the rocker, a hard look on his face. Brody shook his head. "It's a pack of lies, Papa. I wrote in that letter Sarah gave you that the Millers are crooked as they come, and I heard Doc Miller say they framed Ames for the murder of that lady."

Papa looked at Brody. "We didn't know what to believe. You just disappeared."

Mama came to the doorway and reached out to hold Brody's hand. "The little boy keeps asking for his father."

Brody looked at Ames, but he leaned back in the rocker and closed his eyes. "Go on and help dat boy. I just gonna sit back and take me a lil' ol' nap."

Momma tugged on Brody's hand. "I'll bring him some vittles and sweet tea in a bit. Come inside."

Ames cracked an eyelid open. "Thank ye, ma'am."

Inside, the wonderful aroma of stew hung in the air, and Brody's stomach growled. The house was cozy, and he recognized Papa's handiwork in the wooden tables and counters. They weren't highly polished and fancy, but strongly built to last for generations.

He could see Mama's touch, too. Pretty checkered gingham curtains hung from the windows, and a hand-stitched quilt lay over the leather chair in the main room. There were several things from the old cabin that brought back memories.

Brody followed his momma into the bedroom, and they sat on the bed by Todd. He made for a sad sight, just a little lump in the big bed, curled up into a tight ball.

As Brody leaned over him, the bone necklace slipped out of his shirt and fell to the bed. The knot had come untied. The familiar rattle registered with Todd, and he started patting at the covers.

Brody picked it up, wrapped it around Todd's fingers, and placed the turquoise stone in his palm. Todd clenched it.

Looking up, Brody saw his mother watching him. "It was his father's."

Papa stood in the doorway. "Where is his papa?"

Brody softly explained everything he could about what had happened to Todd. As he described the events, Todd pulled the covers over his head and cried.

Momma held a finger up to her mouth, signaling for Brody to stop. "He needs to drink some broth and rest." She left the room, came back with the broth, and managed to spoon a swallow down the boy. He opened his eyes and reached for the cup, drinking it down in great gulps.

Momma pulled the empty cup back and set it and the spoon on the side table. Todd looked up at her and smiled, "Mawme." He put his arms around her and pulled her down, hugging her tightly. Momma climbed on the bed next to him and held Todd close while Brody and Papa eased out of the room.

Brody stepped out onto the porch. Ames opened his eyes and stretched. "Get in here, Ames. I want you to meet my folks proper."

"I best be gettin' on home." Ames rocked forward and groaned a bit as he stood up.

Brody's father came out.

"Papa, this is Ames," Brody said, "the man that saved me on the Devil's Backbone. He's my best friend."

Papa paused before shaking hands with Ames. "I'd like you to stay. Y'all look plum tuckered out, and I want to hear more about this animal that attacked the boy and his father. Come on in." He turned and went inside, holding his ribs on the way to the table. He took a seat and Brody and Ames joined him.

"What happened to your side?" Brody asked.

His father stared at him for a moment but didn't answer. "I can't believe you're back." He took Brody's hand and squeezed. "I swear you have grown a foot."

Momma came into the room and eased the bedroom door shut. "He fell right to sleep. He needs to rest for a while." She sat at the table on the other side of Brody, pulled him over, and kissed his cheek.

After a deep breath, she said, "First thing. We need to know about him." She nodded at Ames. "No offense, but we don't know you and we've heard some pretty terrible things."

"They're not true," Brody said. "Not at all. He saved me, more than once."

"Dat go both ways, lil' feller." Ames looked from Papa to Momma. "Reckon I'd still be on dat mountain if yer boy hadn't come along."

"The things you've heard about us aren't true," Brody said.

"Lawmen have come by several times." Momma reached for Papa's hand. "They said y'all may have murdered that man, and they think you stole some horses."

Papa rubbed Momma's fingers. "The Miller's are offerin' a reward, claiming horse theft and murder."

"We ain't stole nothin', and we ain't done no murder," Ames said.

"Where have you been?" Papa asked Brody. "We have been so worried about you. Your mother is nothing but skin and bones."

"I'm sorry. I got right in the middle of a big mess with some bad people, and didn't want to drag either of you into it."

Momma looked from Brody to Ames. "Just start from the beginning."

"It's a long story. Isn't it, Ames?"

"It is, at dat."

"I can tell you all about it later, but now we have to go find Todd's father, Joe."

Standing and walking to the kitchen, Momma said, "Brody, you've been gone seven months. Your father and I thought you were dead for several of those months. We've got a thousand questions. I think we deserve to hear the whole story."

"Yes, ma'am." He started with his accident in the woods and continued from there, explaining each event in the best detail he could. As he told how Ames had found him and saved his life, Momma came back to the table with some sweet tea and stew.

She set it down in front of Ames and gave him a hug. "I apologize for how I acted earlier. Thank you for helping our son."

Ames gave a big wide grin. Papa reached across the table and shook his hand again. Momma poured tea and brought bowls of stew for everyone.

She sat and held hands with Brody. "We need a family prayer before eating. It's been a long time since we've had one, and we have a lot of things to be thankful for."

Papa took Brody's hand in a strong grip and reached for Momma's. Momma hesitated, then laid her other hand on Ame's. Ames looked down, then up at her in wonder. She smiled.

Papa prayed. When he was finished, Brody continued with the story.

He was hoarse by the time he finished. Papa put his glass down. "We looked for you a long time."

"You came back to the house, didn't you?" Brody asked.

Papa nodded. "More than once."

"I was there one of those times. I thought someone had broken in the house and ran y'all off. So I hid from you by accident."

Momma threw up her hands. "You didn't find the note?"

"Not at first." Brody picked up where he had left off. Ames filled in some of the stories, telling of how the Millers accused him of a murder they committed. They each took turns until reaching the point where they went their separate ways. Brody told of his trapping job with Joseph and Todd, and how something had attacked their camp.

"Oh, that poor little boy," Momma said.

"What do you think it is?" Papa asked Brody.

"I think it's a bear, or something like a bear," he answered. "It makes an awful sound."

"It don't track like no bear," Ames said.

Brody spoke around a mouthful of stew. "Joe took me in and treated me like family. He even offered his help when he found out who I really was. I'm worried he didn't make it."

The conversation grew quiet for a few moments. "He was going to take me to talk to one of the marshals."

"I think that's what you should do," Papa said.

"I don't think so," Momma argued. "They might throw him right in jail."

Papa pushed his empty bowl to the center of the table. "He needs to get this settled. He can't keep running from something he didn't do. That's no way to live."

Momma fidgeted. "Billy swore he would get him. I think it's best if we move away from here and keep him hid."

"You talked to Billy?" Brody asked.

Papa ran his hand through his hair and looked at Momma for a second.

Momma poured him some more tea and nodded. "Tell him."

Papa pulled his glass closer. "He's been by here a few times. The last visit was right after you shot him in the foot."

"What did he want?" Brody asked.

Glancing at Momma, Papa took a drink.

"What happened?" Brody demanded. "What did he do?"

Momma crossed her arms. "His son, Frank, hit your father in the side with an axe handle and nearly broke some ribs."

Chapter Fourteen

Brody buried his face in his hands. "This is all my fault. If I hadn't shot him, this wouldn't have happened."

"They've been by here several times," Papa said, "threatening to do this and that, if we didn't tell them where you were."

Slapping the table, Brody shook his head in frustration. "I should have headed away from Fort Smith and just kept going."

"No," Momma said. "You should have come back long ago."

Papa touched Brody's hand. "Don't you worry. I'll be fine in a few days. There's only one way to stop someone like the Millers. You have to go to the law and explain everything."

"Dat may not stop Billy," Ames said. "He a pure de ol' devil."

"Will you go with me?" Brody asked his father.

"Of course."

"When I get back, we'll go," Brody said.

"When you get back?" Momma frowned.

"I've got to go and look for Joe."

"Absolutely not," she said.

"I have to."

"You said there was something in those woods. I don't want you out there with that killer bear."

"We can report it to the law when we go talk to them," Papa said. "They can go out there and look."

"No," Brody argued. "They might not believe me. They might not be able to find the spot, and I know they won't go right away. I have to leave this evening."

Momma stood and wrung her hands in her apron. Tears formed in her eyes. "I just got you back. I don't think I can handle you leaving again."

"I'm back, Momma, but Todd may never get his daddy back. What if he's still alive? I can't tell Todd we aren't going to look for his father."

"I'm not saying to leave the man out there, just let someone else go."

"What if Ames would have left me, hurt and alone on that mountain?"

Momma put her hands on her hips and looked at his father. "Jim, you need to talk to your boy." Todd called out from the bedroom and she left to check on him.

"Papa," Brody said, "I'm not a boy anymore."

Papa looked at him for a long time. His gaze cut to Ames and then back to Brody. "I don't think it's a good idea. My ribs are hurt, and I couldn't ride a horse to save my life. You shouldn't do this at all, but you sure shouldn't do it alone."

Ames cleared his throat. "I'm goin' as long as we ain't there while it dark."

"We'll leave before dark," Brody said.

"Dat's what ye said last time."

"You need some more people," Papa said. "You need a search party."

While scratching the stubble on his chin, Ames said, "Both of us got reward money hangin' over us. I don't take kindly a bein' in da woods wit a bunch of strangers, and we shore can't go see da law."

The bedroom door opened, and Momma stuck her head out, scowling. She tilted her head toward Brody. *"Flint...* I think Todd wants to see you."

Papa and Ames glanced from Momma to Brody. Papa pushed against the top of the table and struggled to his feet. Brody helped him stand straight and they went to the bedroom.

Todd was sitting up in the bed. His dark hair stuck out in every direction, and the turquoise and bone necklace hung around his neck. He began to cry when Brody sat next to him. "I missed you, Flint."

Rubbing his messy hair, Brody said, "I missed you too. Are you all right?"

"I'm hungry." He wiped his face. "Is Father here?"

"Not yet," Brody said. "I have to go get him."

"Is he outside?"

"He's back at camp."

"When you get him, will you bring back my treasures? I didn't have time to get them."

"What happened?" Brody asked.

"Something was growling. It beat on the shed and broke limbs outside. Father said to run away and meet him at the west trap line. I waited a long, long time before he came and got me."

"Your father came and got you?"

Todd nodded. "He brought me here."

Brody looked to his mother. She shook her head slightly as if telling him not to say anything.

"A bear tried to get us," Todd said. "I don't like bears, Flint." He raised his hand. "I got stickers in my fingers."

"Your hand is shaking."

"I'm real hungry."

"I'll get you something to eat," Momma said, as she left the room.

"She told me she was your mom," Todd said.

"She sure is." Brody hugged him. "I'll be back. I'm going to get something to pick out those thorns."

Joining his mother in the kitchen, he waited for her to say something. She opened the cabinets and rummaged through them, pulling out salve, medicine, and food. She placed each thing on the counter with more force than necessary.

Papa started to say something, but Momma smacked a bowl on the counter so hard they all jumped. He closed his mouth, and motioned for Ames to follow him outside.

After the door closed, Momma turned to her son. "So, you've changed your name to Flint?"

"Only with Joe and Todd. I had to change it."

She stared at him and carefully reached out to move his hair away from the scar on his forehead. Her gentle finger traced along the rough skin. Tears trailed down her face. "My little boy isn't so little anymore."

"But I'll always be your little boy, Momma."

She pulled him to her and shook with each sob. Wrapping his arms around her, he hugged her tightly.

Momma let him go and cleared her throat. "I don't even have to bend over to hug you anymore. Listen, I know you want to go look for his father right now, but I want you to wait for a few days."

Brody opened his mouth to protest, but she talked over him.

"Your father will be well enough to ride in a week or so. Then he can go with you to look for Joe, and then y'all can go see the law." Her expression was set.

Not wanting to start an argument, he simply hugged her.

Brody watched Todd eat and tried to keep him calm while Momma picked stickers from his hands with a needle. After it was over, he curled up in the covers and fell asleep again.

His mother decided her boy still looked hungry, so she cooked up some sweet cornbread and turnip greens. Ames and Brody did their best to fatten up. It gave him a much-needed surge of energy. Even though his eyes felt puffy from not getting but a few catnaps earlier, he was ready to set out for Indian Territory.

"Did you see my horse?" he asked Momma.

"I did. Where did you get it?"

"I bought it from the undertaker."

Mama smiled. "You didn't name him Lucky, did you?"

"His name's Buck and he's a fine horse." Wrinkles ran from the corners of her eyes and mouth, and most were surely caused by his absence. Knowing he was about to cause her more grief broke his heart. "Speaking of that, Ames, we better go take care of Buck and your mule.

Ames frowned. "Dis is some fine cornbread. Best I ever had."

"You can come back and finish when we are done."

Ames looked to Momma. "Ma'am, could I carry me a piece outside?"

"That would be fine. I'm glad you like it." Momma looked pleased.

They walked around the corner of the house toward the corral. Ames took a bite of the bread. A large piece fell off. "Here, hold dis." He held the remaining cornbread toward Brody.

Brody took it and watched Ames bend over. He picked up the pieces of crumbled bread and collected them in his hand.

Wrinkling his eyebrows, Brody asked, "What are you doing?"

Ames picked grass and debris out of the bits of cornbread.

"You're not going to eat that, are you?"

Ames blew into his palm. "I ain't wastin' it."

"But it's dirty."

Ames popped the bread into his mouth.

Brody scrunched up his face. "I could see dirt on it. You ate dirt. That's nasty." Brody handed the rest of the cornbread back to Ames.

"I learnt my lesson years ago," Ames said. "Nearly got my hind end beat off for wastin' food. Ma cooked some awful biscuits, and I hid mine in da bushes. Later, she ask if I liked it and I lied, even smacked da lips and rubbed da belly."

Brody laughed. "You got a whipping. She knew you were telling a fib."

"Dat ol' farm hound brought dat hard biscuit 'round and when Ma saw him chewin' on it, she dusted da seat of my pants real good fer wastin' food." Ames ate the last piece of cornbread and smiled.

Shaking his head, Brody turned around and walked away. "You are a nut. Come on, we got to get the horses."

"We leavin', ain't we?" Ames asked.

"We have to. I can't leave Joe out there."

"Yer folks gonna be mighty upset," Ames warned.

Reaching for the gate on the pen, Brody paused. "It's the right thing to do. Todd doesn't have a mother. Joe's the only person he has."

"He has you," Ames said, "and you is da finest friend anybody could ever have."

Brody turned to give Ames a big smile, but then he saw Papa standing behind them.

"Brody is a fine friend," Papa said. "He's also the best son any father could have. I know you're leaving and I'd like to stop you but the truth is, I can't. I was off on my on when I was younger than you, running cattle all the way to the sale, buying and selling as I went. I felt grown when I was twelve. I shouldn't expect any less from you at fifteen."

Leaning against the fence, Brody put his hands in his pockets. "I don't feel very grown up sometimes."

Papa came over to him. "You're doing fine. We just need to get this all straightened out. Brody, there's over a hundred people in that tiny jail in Fort Smith. I don't' want you being one of 'em."

"Joe is friends with one of the marshals. All of us can go talk to him when I get back." He looked toward the house. "Did you tell Momma I was leaving?"

"She knows."

"She knows?"

"She sent me out here to go with you."

"I wish you could, Papa, I really do but your hurt and we can't leave Momma and Todd here alone."

"I know. I wouldn't want the Millers coming back without me here."

"So, what are we going to do?" Brody asked.

"I'm going to stay here and you're leaving."

"Does Momma know that?"

Papa shook his head. "She thinks I'm going with you."

"Should I go say goodbye to her?" Brody started toward the house.

Reaching out, Papa took hold of his arm, stopping him. "She said she could not handle letting you go and to make sure you come back."

"She's going to be mad at you for not going," Brody said.

"I know." Papa opened the gate.

Brody brought Buck out. Ames followed with his mule, and Papa shut the gate back. He opened the door to the barn. Holding his ribs, Papa reached for a saddle sitting across the top rail of a stall. He tried to lift it with one arm but couldn't.

"This will be a lot easier on him and your hind end," Papa said.

Ames grabbed it and helped him pull it down. He tossed the saddle across Buck's back and Brody started fastening the straps.

"I'll bring it back when I'm done," he said.

Laughing, Papa wrapped the reins around the saddle horn. "It's yours anyway."

"Mine?"

"I bought it with some of the money you left us." He put a hand on Brody's shoulder. "In that letter, you said the money was given to you from a friend."

Brody pointed at Ames.

Ames smiled. "Yep, he been da best friend. Gave him half of it."

Papa paused. His gaze shifted from Ames to Brody.

"It wasn't stolen," Brody said, trying to reassure him.

Papa relaxed and squeezed Brody's shoulder as he let go. "I didn't want to spend any of it but we had to. I was just worried about using it."

"I left it for you to use," Brody said.

"We do have some bills to pay."

"That's what it's for. Use it, Papa. I don't want y'all suffering anymore."

Papa grinned. "Get on out of here."

Brody climbed up. "The saddle feels good. It's much better."

They rode along the side of the house and Papa walked behind. He stopped at the corner and waved. Brody waved back, glancing at the front porch, hoping Momma would be there but she wasn't.

"Circle south of town," Papa said. "When you get back, we'll get with the law and work this all out."

"Yes, sir," Brody said over his shoulder.

As they left, his heart ached. It felt so good to see his folks again. He could hardly believe he was leaving, but he couldn't live with himself if he didn't at least look for Joseph.

They would have to stop before dark and get some rest. The next morning they would need to get up early, ride to the trapping camp and start looking. It would be important to find him quickly. Brody didn't ever want to be caught in those woods after dark again.

Chapter Fifteen

Taking his father's advice, Brody and Ames skirted the edge of town and eased their way back into Indian Territory. It took longer, but they avoided the busy streets and prying eyes.

The afternoon was warm, and Buck's stride rocked Brody back and forth. His eyelids drooped and his head wobbled. Jerking awake, Brody looked over to Ames. "I'm sleepy."

"We needs ta camp soon," Ames said. "I'm hurtin' and worn to da bone."

"Just a couple more hours and we can stop about ten miles from the camp."

Ames chuckled. "May have ta wrap some rope around me ta keep from fallin' out of dis saddle."

The trip lingered on and both of them fought to stay awake. They stayed in the woods as much as possible, and Brody felt he must have fallen asleep at least a dozen times.

Reaching an old grown up trail, Ames stopped his mule. "How about here?"

"It looks good to me," Brody said.

They set up camp and fell into their bedrolls early, long before sunset. Brody wanted to worry about the search they would go on the next day, but he fell asleep as soon as he hit the ground.

Ames shook him awake the next morning. Brody felt sure he could have slept another hundred days. Around mid-morning, they arrived at camp and Brody jumped down from Buck's back. The grasshoppers were already buzzing as they leapt from the ground to escape his feet.

Ames got down and stretched his arms into the air, then reached down and rubbed his knee. "Don't know how long dis old leg gonna hold out."

"Can we ride the horses to where you lost Joe's trail?" Brody asked hopefully.

"Don't think so," Ames said. "A quarter mile back der we have ta cut north, and it drop off real steep. It ain't no place ta be ridin' a horse."

They put the mule and horse on the tie-out, next to the shed, and checked their guns. Brody made sure his rifle was fully loaded.

With weapons in hand and packs over their backs, they headed into the woods. After a half hour, the trail cut to the north. The terrain kept falling away the farther they traveled, and soon they reached a drop off. Using trees to keep his balance, Brody slid down the steep hill. The ground leveled off as they walked through a grove of holly trees.

"Dey's a little cliff up here," Ames said.

"Can we get down?" Brody asked.

Ames laughed. "I got down it. I reckon we can do it again."

Jumping onto the large rocks, dead moss crunched under Brody's feet. He went to the edge and looked over. "It's not too far down."

"Be careful," Ames warned. "Don't want ye gettin' no broke bones."

Brody stepped down to a large boulder and then jumped to another. Leaping down again, he landed on the ground. Ames followed but much more carefully and without jumping. He slid down each boulder until reaching the bottom.

"Da creek is down dat way."

As they reached the stream, Brody noticed how small it was. "Is this where you lost the trail?"

"Somewhere right here." Ames picked up a beaver stick and used it like a cane. Beavers had chewed the bark from the sturdy, green limb, leaving it straight and smooth.

The creek was less than six feet wide. Smooth rocks littered the middle of it, and water slowly squeezed its way between them. Large oaks had grown along the banks of the stream, and the rolling water had exposed their twisted roots.

"We're not going to find any blood," Brody said. "That big rain washed all the sign away."

"Dey was a lot of blood, Brody. I just don't think he made it."

"Did you look on the other side?"

Kneeling next to the creek, Ames swished his hand in the water and rubbed it on his face. "I looked all over da place."

Brody sat on a rock to rest for a moment. "You said he was bleeding pretty bad. It couldn't have stopped all of a sudden, could it?"

Jabbing at the ground with his stick, Ames looked downstream. "If somethin' were trailing me, I might try goin' down da creek."

"It would hide his tracks, and the blood would get washed away. We should take a look."

Ames crossed the water, and they walked along the stream, Brody on one side and Ames on the other. While looking for anything out of the ordinary, Brody started thinking about the evening they had found the dying man. He remembered how the fellow had only been wearing his long johns and a coat, and how Buck had been bareback.

"That man we found. This thing attacked him in the middle of the night too. Just like it did Joe and Todd."

"Ye think so?"

"He didn't have time to get dressed and saddle Buck. He just jumped on the horse and rode till he got away. Then he must have tied Buck to a tree and died from his wounds."

Ames looked at him from across the creek. "What ye thinkin'?"

"Joe's horses," Brody said. "They are gone, but Todd and Joe didn't take them."

Ames stopped walking. "You reckon dat bear-thing run 'em off?"

"They would have come back to camp. That's where we fed them."

"Maybe dey got ate up."

"Two full grown horses, and no sign of blood or bones?"

Ames started walking again. "Well, maybe not, but dey's spring growth all over da place. Dem horses could be out grazing fer days."

"We didn't look for horse tracks," Brody said. "We should go back and check."

"Dat rain were a gully washer," Ames said. "Dey ain't no tracks ta be had."

"Joe's horses were bigger than Buck. Their tracks would be deep. I bet we can still find them."

"Why ye wantin' ta track dem, Brody? We know Joe came down ta dis creek."

Brody stepped over a dead tree. "But maybe he whistled one of his horses down here and rode it out."

"Ain't no horse coming down dem rocks."

"But what if he walked down the creek for a while and then climbed back up the hill and found one of the horses."

"He were hurt too bad. We gonna stay on dis stream a little longer."

Brody kept going, looking and hoping to find Joseph sitting on a stump. Not finding any sign at all was even more worrisome than finding a blood trail, and wishful thinking would get them nowhere.

The creek turned and twisted and after another hour of walking, Brody's feet were hurting, and he noticed Ames was leaning more and more on his makeshift cane. "You ready for a rest?"

Ames wiped his brow. "Sure am."

Pointing to a series of boulders sticking out of the water, Brody said, "Can you make it across there to this side?"

Ames started across, using the beaver stick to keep his balance. He carefully stepped from rock to rock and as he reached the last one, he stopped. "Dey's blood right here."

Brody took several quick steps and then stopped. His stomach lurched. "Right here, too."

Stretching from the boulder to the bank, Ames struggled to keep his footing. "Found some more. It's awful fresh."

Brody ran a short ways away from the noise of the water. He leaned back and bellowed with all his might, "Jo-o-o-o-e!"

They listened. Brody tried again, "Jo-o-o-o-e!"'"

Ames gave an ear-splitting whistle.

The woods were silent. All they could hear was the gurgling of the creek.

Ames motioned for Brody to keep following the spots of blood. The splatter of red led them to a worn game trail. Ames and Brody took turns calling out for Joseph.

When the signs of blood disappeared from the trail, Ames stopped Brody. "Dey ain't no more blood. He must have left da path. Let's start a small circle and work our way out. I'll look over here. You circle dat way."

Easing into the thicker woods, Brody studied the ground closely. The larger trees had blocked out too much sun, which kept grass from growing below. Brush had filled between the trees and he had to push through the undergrowth. He reached a tiny clearing, no more than ten feet across. In the middle of the spot was a splash of blood.

"Over here," Brody said.

Ames came in from the side. "Dey's a smaller trail right here. It's comin' off dat big one."

"Any sign?"

"Just a couple specks."

"There's some big spots here in the middle of this clearing," Brody said.

Ames shuffled over.

"Is your leg hurting bad?" Brody asked.

"Gonna hafta rest soon." Ames stepped past him and to the other side. A pile of dead brush was on the left. As Ames went around it and stepped into the woods, something cracked loudly. Stumbling back, he fell to the ground.

Brody was there in a flash. "Ames. What happened?" He raised his gun but couldn't see anything to aim at. "What was that?"

Ames got back to his feet. "Looky there."

The beaver stick Ames had been using as a cane, was still standing upright. A large bear trap was clamped tight around the bottom of the limb. The pressure of the jaws had nearly cut the stick in half.

"Yer friend set him a trap fer dat thing following him."

Brody squatted down by it. "That's not one of Joe's traps. We didn't have anything nearly that big."

Ames grabbed a sapling and used it to pull himself up. He brushed his pants off. "You fer sure about dat?"

"I've set and checked all of his traps, even boiled the scent off of 'em. There weren't any like that." Brody grabbed the stick and wiggled it.

Ames glanced around. "Hold on, Brody. Don't be movin' around."

"Why not?"

"Somebody set dis trap fer us."

"For us?"

"Whoever done dis is tryin' ta catch a man. Don't be movin' 'round."

"You think there's more?" Brody asked.

Ames nodded. "You see dat pile of brush and how dat long dead limb is laying on de other side?"

"I see it."

"Dey set dat up. We gonna hafta back out of here."

Brody stared at Ames. "We can't give up on Joe's trail. I won't do it."

"Dis ain't his trail. Look over der."

To the right, Brody saw something furry and bloody in the underbrush. "Is that a rabbit?"

Ames pulled on the walking stick, snapping it into at the weak point where the jaws had clamped down on it. "Don't move." Jabbing at the ground with the limb, Ames made his way to the carcass.

Using the stick, he prodded at the bloody animal and rolled it closer. "Dat's what it is. Somebody use dis ta make dat blood trail."

Brody had watched Joseph set his traps. He would place rocks and limbs in certain spots, to make sure the animal he was hunting would be forced to place its feet exactly where he wanted.

Ames was right. The spot they had walked into was a man sized set. The blood trail, the brush pile, and the dead limb had funneled them straight to the trap.

Looking toward the main trail, Brody wondered how many more traps were hiding in the leaves and pine needles. Ames moved ahead, sweeping at the ground with the limb as he went. Brody stayed close and expected another trap to bite the stick at any moment.

"What are you doing, Ames?"

Ames stopped on the trail and got down on his hands and knees again. Placing his head close to the dirt, he looked sideways at the ground. "We needs ta get on out a here."

Brody knew he was right. Whether Joseph set that trap or not, they were in danger. Ames had spent years living on the mountain, trapping and hunting to survive. He had been alone so long he may have gone a little crazy, but he knew how to read a trail the way some folks read a book.

They kept silent most of the way as they backtracked, with Ames going first. Using long, stout sticks, they prodded anything that looked suspicious. The more Brody thought about the trap, the more he convinced himself Joseph had found it and made the set for what was after him.

When they reached the horses, Ames was limping badly. He cleared his throat and climbed on the mule. "Let's get on back ta where we camped last night. It'll be black as pitch soon, and I hafta think fer a while."

"I need to go back, Ames. We've been over that trail twice and didn't find anymore traps. You go rest, and I'm going to go back."

"An' folks say I be crazy," Ames muttered. "Get yer backside on dat leather, 'fore I knock a knot on yer durn head."

Giving up on the argument, Brody climbed onto Buck's back. While they rode, Brody glanced back often. He couldn't stop the feeling that something was watching them.

Chapter Sixteen

They arrived at their campsite from the previous evening. Ames sat and leaned against a boulder while Brody built a fire.

He rubbed his sore leg. "I done messed up. Messed up bad."

"What is it?"

"We ain't huntin' Joe. Dey's somebody huntin' us. Dat trap were meant to catch one o' us. There's evil out der, and it ain't no animal."

Brody fanned the growing flames. "What I heard in the woods sounded like some kind of monster bear."

"Oh, it are a monster," Ames said. "But it a man o' some sort."

"You said the tracks were strange," Brody said.

"Dey were."

"And what about those claw marks?"

Ames didn't answer.

"Joe could have set that trap." Brody couldn't help saying it. "It wasn't meant for us."

"Ye said he ain't got no traps dat big."

"Maybe he found it," Brody argued. "He could have came across an old trap and set it up for that monster that attacked them."

Ames did not look convinced. "Weren't nary a speck a rust on dem jaws. Don't ye reckon it strange?"

"I don't know, Ames. But we should have stayed. Joe could have been around the next corner."

"Lil' feller, I knowed ye got yer heart set on findin' dat Indian boy's daddy but ye better start thinkin' wit yer noggin or we gonna get hurt. Or worse."

The night was closing in on them. Brody hung his head. The wind picked up, rustling through the trees, and off in the distance a pack of coyotes started singing. Eerie howls rose in volume as others joined in. He shuddered. "I don't want to be out there when it gets dark."

"We look again tomorrow," Ames said.

Brody took some food from his pack. "I'm sorry for getting you into this."

"Naw," Ames said. He stood and stretched, holding his arms up high as if trying to reach the towering treetops. "Dis is where I belong. I been feelin' like my old self since we been traveling again. Don't think ol' Ames ever gonna be a good farmer."

"I thought that's what you wanted to do."

Ames leaned against the rock. "Don't much know what I want to be anymore."

"What's wrong?"

Leaning against a tree, Ames stuck his hands in his pockets. "I ain't never been nothin'. Ain't never been good at nothin'."

"You're a great tracker," Brody said.

Ames rubbed his face. "Can't stick with nothin' long enough ta get good at it. Dem old thoughts won't stay gone."

"What thoughts?"

Ames looked out into the woods and then to Brody. "How I ran and hid and didn't fight fer dem boys."

"The battle?" Brody asked. "We already talked about this. I don't think you were a coward. You weren't even a soldier. You were just there, trying to earn some money."

"Ain't no man should act dat way." Ames sat on the ground and reached inside his pack. He brought out some cornbread and handed Brody a piece.

Brody took it. "You have to let those things go. You didn't do anything wrong, and you sure aren't no coward." Brody spoke in the same tone he had heard Papa use. "You need to leave those troubles behind you. I don't want you to think about it again. You hear me?"

Upon hearing Brody's angry voice, Ames grew real still. His eyebrows rose for a moment, but then he broke into laughter. "You gonna make a good daddy someday."

They both chuckled, and Brody was relieved to see Ames light-hearted again.

After supper, they went to bed. Brody was tired, but he couldn't let go of his worries. His thoughts kept taking him back to the creature in the woods. It was huge and hairy, and it stunk like rotting meat. It growled like no other animal he had ever heard. And it was utterly terrifying.

Ames seemed to think it was a man, but there was no way this could be true. It had to be some sort of devil-bear.

Brody shuddered. He got up and put more wood on the fire, huddling close to it. Indians were tough, and Joseph was as tough as they come. If anyone could survive against a devil-bear, it was him.

The next morning, they went back to the stream and cautiously followed it farther. Ames whispered to Brody, telling him to step carefully and not speak.

He stayed behind Ames and watched him work his tracking skills. He spent more time on his knees than on his feet, even though it was hurting him. Inspecting every rock and spot of soil, he inched along at a slug's pace.

Motioning him over, Ames pointed at a large oval smudge on the ground. Brody looked it over. "What is it?"

Ames shushed him by holding a finger to his lips. After creeping along for hours, they stopped long enough to eat some dried meat. Brody tried to whisper again, but Ames frowned and shook his head.

The painfully slow process continued for another two hours. Ames leaned against a tree and rubbed his bad leg. Brody sat on a flat rock and waited. A breeze came up the creek, bringing the scent of smoke. Ames must have smelled it too. Reaching over, he grabbed Brody's sleeve and pulled him to his feet.

Farther down, the creek dropped off between a set of massive boulders, and the water crashed against the rocks about ten feet below. Ames started down on the right, picking his way slowly.

Brody was right behind him. Ames gasped and jerked back into Brody, causing him to have to grab a root to keep his balance. Using his walking stick, Ames slung something off the rock and into the trees. He looked over his shoulder, his eyes wide and panicked, and mouthed *snake!* Brody groaned. It wasn't as if they didn't have enough things scaring the daylights out of them.

They were both jumpy when they reached the bottom. Moss-covered slabs of rock rose up on one side of the creek. Old trees were rotting on the ground on the other side and had been overgrown with a dense tangle of vines and thorns. A steep mountain face was behind it blocking any direct sunlight, making the draw gloomy. Goosebumps covered Brody's arms.

Ames pointed at the water's edge. There were scuffmarks on the rocks. In the dirt right by the edge of the water was part of a hoof print.

Cocking his musket, Ames started down the draw. Brody gripped his rifle tightly and followed on the huge slabs of rock that ran along the creek bed. The canyon had Brody spooked, but with the rocky terrain at least they wouldn't have to worry about stepping into a steel trap.

The air was stagnant and putrid. Up ahead and to the side of the trail, was a deer carcass. The backstraps and hams were gone, but the rest was rotting. They eased past it, disturbing the blowflies. Ames stopped and met Brody's eyes. He pointed at his feet and put his finger across his lips again.

The muscles in Brody's legs quivered. Every good sense he had was telling him to back out of this place and leave.

They came to a spot where the steep rock walls pinched the hollow down to a narrow pass, less than a hundred steps across. The smell of smoke grew stronger.

Something snorted, frightening Brody so badly that he nearly dropped his gun. Ames pointed the musket toward the noise. When Brody recovered from the scare, he saw it was a brown and white paint horse that had made the sound. It was tied to a picket line about twenty steps from the creek, and he recognized the animal right away.

Ames turned to him with a questioning look.

"Joe's," Brody mouthed with hardly a sound.

Just past the horse, they entered the narrow pass. Ames stopped abruptly. When he didn't move, Brody leaned so he could see around him and was astounded.

Several open traps hung from the branches of a tree in front of them. The next tree had more. Looking farther out, Brody could see there were blackened traps hanging from all of them.

Some hung on chains at face height, some low enough to catch a knee. There were hundreds at different heights. The jaws were open, and they slowly swiveled in the light breeze. Brody had never seen anything so deadly and ominous in all his life.

Finally, Ames leaned close to Brody's ear. His voice was a rough whisper. "We can't climb dem rock walls. We gotta go through."

He turned sideways and squeezed between two dangling traps.

Glancing at the sea of gently swaying jaws, Brody could see that all of their pans were flat. Looking closely, he saw the latches had been filed down. They were set on hair triggers and ready to snap at the slightest touch. There were traps of all sizes, huge bear traps with sharp teeth, medium sized wolf and cat traps, and smaller ones for foxes and raccoons. The smooth jaws on the smaller traps had been altered. Someone had filed jagged teeth in the metal.

"Don't touch 'em," he whispered.

He started forward but froze as he noticed a number three coyote trap with its jaws wrapped around a dead woodpecker. Most of the bird's feathers had fallen to the ground and blowflies buzzed in the air.

Ames worked his way to the right and then reversed direction, until he was far to the left. Bending low, he motioned for Brody to come over.

Brody stepped from rock to rock, making sure he didn't place his foot where a trap could be hiding. Something brushed the brim of his hat. He turned his head slowly to see a trap twisting in the air beside his head. His heart thumped in a wild rhythm. In front of him were two more hanging close to the ground. He sucked in his stomach and eased between them.

The edge of a jaw caught his shirt and turned slowly. Brody's eyes grew wide, and he stopped dead until the trap became still. Taking a deep breath, he inched through the gap and finally reached Ames.

Leaning close to his ear, Ames lowered his voice, "Dey is a more open path here. Wait 'til I get clear 'fore ya follow."

He stayed on the rocky trail, ducking and bending low to avoid the jaws, especially the toothy bear traps. Brody spotted another one that had snapped onto a dead limb that had fallen in it.

Brody looked past the forest of jaws. The land opened up more and sloped upward through some thinning trees. There was a small, rickety cabin. Smoke trailed out of its leaning chimney. Attached to the cabin was an old split-log fence, and three horses were inside it.

Brody knew for sure he had been fooled. There was no monster. No creature had torn up the woods with Joseph's trap. It wasn't an Indian legend or wampus cat. It was a man who had done all of this.

Letting anger get the best of him, Brody started forward. He was determined to help Joseph if he was being held in the cabin. The barrel of the Henry clanged against one of the hanging traps.

Brody cringed as it swayed wildly. He started to reach for it, but pulled back in time. The contraption collided with another trap and set off a series of snapping jaws. The traps swung around as they clamped tight, setting off others.

It was as if the trees had started to dance. Metal teeth clamped, causing traps to jerk, the rattling of the chains punctuated with loud *thwaks*.

Ames dropped to the ground. "Get down!"

Brody fell flat just as a bear trap set off, snapping inches above his head.

The assault of loud metallic snaps and rattles was deafening, and spiraled out in waves.

As the cacophony began to ebb, something large and hairy ran from behind the cabin.

Ames scrambled past the last traps and shot.

A man, covered with furs, threw a knife toward Ames. Ames ducked and the knife flew by harmlessly. They could see the man weave among the boulders and trees as he ran.

"Are you all right?" Brody yelled.

"Ain't hurt none," Ames growled back, as he reloaded.

Brody quickly crawled forward under the swinging metal, afraid to stand up in case a trap was still set. When he reached Ames, he stood up, and they circled the cabin, finding a bizarre collection of things.

Underneath a stretched canvas were stacks of furs as tall as a man. Next to them was a pile of traps and a large barrel he must have been using to boil them. There was a lean-to shed attached to the back of the house, and underneath it were at least six saddles and leather tack. Brody's heart dropped. One of the saddles was Joseph's.

Brody spotted an open door to the cabin and stuck his head in. It had only one room that he could see. There were at least a dozen knives lying on a table. A pile of pots and pans had been stacked in the corner. Rusty guns were leaned against the wall.

"Get over here," he said. "Take a look." Brody's anger rose. "That shotgun is Joe's."

"Leave it fer now. Dat big feller is gonna tell us everything when I gets done. I seen him stumble. I think I hit him."

They headed in the direction the man had gone, still wary of traps.

"He's been killing people and stealing their stuff," Brody said.

"Uh huh. I hope he's hit good cause my leg ain't gonna hold out."

They found broken stalks in the brush and roughed-up ground. Ames didn't have to get on his knees to track. The path was clear as could be.

"He flat out runnin'," Ames said.

After they had gone about a quarter of a mile, Brody saw a spot of blood on a holly leaf. "Here, Ames. Here's some blood."

"I knowed I hit him." Ames led the way, but the trail started up the side of the tall ridge. Stumbling, he kept his balance by holding onto the trees. He finally went to his knees and grabbed at his leg.

Brody came up beside him. "I'll help you."

"No, just let me rest fer a bit."

"We can't let him get away, Ames. He may have Joe tied up somewhere."

At the top of the ridge, Brody saw the man slip between two big trees. He was almost doubled over and holding his stomach. "There he goes." Brody took off, running up the hill.

"Come back here," Ames called.

Chapter Seventeen

B rody leaned forward and dug into the ground with each stride.
He could hear Ames yelling for him, but Brody knew he could
catch the wounded man. He wouldn't stop until he knew what had
happened to Joseph.

When he reached the tree, he found a splatter of blood. A smear
of red marked the bark of the next pine he came to. Brody caught a
glimpse of his quarry, again, almost at the top of the ridge.

Brody dashed toward the top but lost sight of him among the
trees and boulders where it flattened out at the top. Keeping his gun
ready, he stepped out into a small clearing. Ten steps farther was a
cliff's edge.

There was a large bloody handprint on a sapling growing right at
the edge. Keeping his gun ready, he eased close and looked over.

The height caused a thrill in his stomach, and he quickly
stepped back. He suspected that the man thought about going over
the lip, but the drop was way too far to survive. A wide swirling
creek was at the bottom, and there was no sign of a body.

He went back to the tree and looked some more. He found a tiny
wet spot on the rocky ground, maybe a drop of sweat. A couple of
steps past a rocky outcropping, there was a definite blood trail. After
a few feet, the stone gave way to soil, and he could make out the
same strange track that had mystified them at camp. Brody looked
ahead.

"Oh, no."

A wall of rock was on the left, the cliff's edge on the right, and tangle of brush in the middle.

It was a funnel, a trap.

A shadow crossed him. He dove to the right. The fur-covered man jumped from a ledge above, landed in a crouch, and immediately sprang forward. Brody rolled away, just as the man swiped at his face with two metal claws.

Brody leaped to his feet, but the Henry slipped out of his fingers and dropped to the ground. He bent down and grabbed it. The killer lunged for him. Stumbling back, Brody shot and missed.

 The man smacked the gun away with his arm. A loud metallic clang sounded as an iron cuff around his wrist collided with the barrel. Dropping the rifle, Brody frantically tried to keep his footing.

A bloody hand grabbed for him, but Brody was on the move. He reached for his gun, which was lying on the ground.

The man's fingers snagged his shirt, and with one arm he yanked Brody's face up next to his. Greasy strings of hair covered much of his forehead and eyebrows. A matted, dirty beard hid his mouth and chin. His exposed cheeks were scarred and stained with soil, and he reeked of rotten meat and blood.

The wild-man raised a hand, and Brody saw his fingers squeezed through two rings that made up the handle of his claw-like blades. Another iron cuff was on this wrist. A few links of chain dangled from it. He pressed the blade tips against Brody's throat and snarled, "She is mine!"

Brody slammed his fist into the man's bleeding belly. He felt a sting on his throat, as the man threw back his head and bellowed. Brody raised his hands between the man's arms and clapped him on his ears as hard as he could. The man dropped him and groaned. Brody ran faster than a jackrabbit.

Looking back, he saw the layers of furs bouncing as the madman came after him in a fury.

"Ames!" Brody screamed.

He turned his head forward a second too late. He smacked into the boulder so hard he was disoriented. The wild-man was on him seconds later, pushing him against the hard rock. The sharp blades flashed as the man lifted them high to strike. Brody shifted at the last moment as the knives slammed into the boulder.

The force of the blow twisted the man's fist at the wrist, and he yelled in pain. He opened his fingers and shook his hand. The double bladed knife fell in the dirt.

Brody pushed off from the boulder, but the man was too quick. He used his forearm across Brody's chest to pin him back against the boulder again.

Desperate, Brody used the heel of his boot to stomp down on the shapeless leather wrapped around the man's feet. The man hollered out but didn't release the pressure.

The killer tried to choke him with his free hand but his grip was weak and he winced with pain. Brody knew the man's fingers must have broken when he stabbed the boulder, so he yanked on them with both hands.

The man yelled and his rancid breath hit Brody square in the face. Brody brought his knee up hard, hitting the killer between the legs. The madman hunched over and moaned.

He lunged forward, but the man slugged him in the side of the head. Everything turned dark, and he fell to the ground, setting off a hidden trap. The pressure and pain, tight on his heel, brought him back around.

Brody saw that a heavy bear trap had barely caught him, closing mostly on the back of his boot heel and the thick leather just above it. Even so, his foot ached terribly.

The man crouched a few feet away and panted with a raspy growl. He held his hand tightly across his belly. Blood dripped steadily between his fingers.

Scrambling to his feet, Brody tried to run, but the trap got in the way. The wild-man roared and came after him. Suddenly, the killer tripped over the chain on the trap and barreled into Brody, sending them tumbling over the edge of the cliff.

Brody jerked to a stop and was flipped upside down with great force. The madman managed to grab the chain, and his body slammed into Brody's.

Glancing at the trap, Brody could see the grapple had caught on something. He tried pushing the man away but the weight proved to be too much and the hooks did not hold. Falling freely for another foot, Brody cried out in fear.

They jolted to a stop. Pain ran down Brody's leg as his muscles were stretched to their limits. As they swung back and forth, Brody could see the wild-man's hand wrapped around the chain just above the trap. A few feet above, the grapple had caught in a tree root. "Ames! Help me!"

"She is mine!" the man howled, blood and spittle flying out with each word.

"Where's Joe?" Brody demanded.

The killer's nasty beard hid all of the features of his face except for his dirty cheeks and fevered amber eyes. Those evil eyes narrowed and he turned to look up.

He began to climb and moaned in pain each time he used his wounded hand. Wrapping his legs around Brody's waist, he was able to get a better purchase on the chain.

The shifting weight pulled at the tendons in Brody's leg, and he yelled in pain. His foot slipped loose from the boot a tiny bit.

He tried reaching for the killer, but the man had already worked his way up far enough to get a hand over the edge and around the sapling. When the stretching weight lifted, Brody was relieved, but as he watched the man, his blood ran cold.

The killer groaned loudly as he pulled his body up, got to his feet, and then looked down at Brody. "You never take her." Reaching for the grapple, he jerked and twisted it.

"No!" Brody yelled. "Stop it!"

His eyes grew wide with horror. The man strained to pull the hooks up and free of the root. Brody closed his eyes and prayed, waiting to be dropped.

A deep boom roared at the top of the cliff, and the chain jolted as the grapple caught on the root again. He could hear sounds of a scuffle. Ames and the wild-man careened into view.

Swinging with all his might, Ames tried hitting the man with the smoking musket. The killer grabbed the gun and Ames punched him. Both men grunted with effort as they struggled with each other, pushing and shoving.

The men teetered on the edge, and Brody gasped, thinking they would tumble over any second. Instead, they fell away from the cliff and out of sight.

Moments later, gravel and dirt cascaded down. Brody turned away, protecting his eyes. As he looked back, a flailing body shot past him, speeding toward the ground below. Although Brody couldn't see, he heard a loud smack against the earth. It happened so fast, he wasn't sure if it was Ames or the killer.

More dirt crumbled and fell from the cliff's edge.

Brody whispered over and over, "Please be Ames, please be Ames, please be Ames…"

A dreadful silence followed, until Brody heard the distinct sound of ripping fabric. As his pant leg tore, the heel of his boot popped over the back of his foot, and he slipped a couple of inches.

An arm reached over the edge, grabbing the chain. "Ye all right, lil' feller?" Ames looked down at him. "Are ye hurt?"

"I will be if my pants rip anymore," Brody choked out. "My foot is slipping out of my boot."

Ames took a tight grip, grunted with effort, and pulled at the grapple and chain. Brody pushed against the side of the cliff, trying to help as much as he could. Wheezing with each breath, Ames slowly inched him up. When strong, calloused hands finally grabbed his leg, Brody felt safe.

With a big heave, Ames pulled him over the edge and they both flopped on the ground. "Ye purt near scared me ta death."

"Scared you?" Brody said. "I thought I was going to die. Several times. Think I'm going to need a new pair of drawers for sure."

Ames grinned at him. "It were a close one." He sat up and rubbed his bad leg. His grin faded and he winced.

"Are you hurt?" Brody asked.

"Dat furry devil hit me with my own gun. So, I just kicked him and over da edge he went." He eyed the blood on Brody's clothes. "Dat yourn or his?"

"His. Your shot hit him in the stomach, and he lost a lot of blood." Brody leaned over the edge.

Looking down the cliff, he spotted a rocky ledge about halfway down. A bloody smear on its edge told him the madman had hit the outcropping on the way down. The man's body lay in the edge of a rolling creek at the bottom of the cliff. He was on his back and his face was a mess. A ribbon of red spread out beneath him and into the water.

Brody couldn't speak for a moment. Yet again, he was looking at a dead man. He swallowed hard. "That man wasn't right in the head, and he didn't tell me anything about Joe. He just wanted to kill me."

Ames got up and his leg almost buckled. He caught his balance and started prying at the jaws of the trap, still attached to Brody's boot and pants.

"We lucky dis here trap is missin' a spring. Ain't no way we could get 'er open if it had both of 'em." Ames stood with both feet on the long flat spring sticking out the side of the trap. The metal eye lowered, allowing the jaws to open.

Brody gently pulled his foot and pants free. "Thanks, Ames. He had me believing there was a monster in these woods."

"He were a monster, as close ta one as I ever seen. He been hidin' out here fer many a year. Ye see how he filed teeth in all dem traps? Dat took a long time."

Brody took his boot the rest of the way off and rubbed his calf and heel. "I think he's killed a lot of folks. He said something about a woman. Said we couldn't take her."

"What ye think he meant?" Ames stepped off the spring and the jaws snapped shut.

The sound made Brody shudder. "I don't know."

Ames eyeballed the trap for a moment, stepped to the edge, and then flung it over the cliff. He peered after it. "Dat creek done washed him off."

Brody looked over the edge. "He's gone?"

"Water took him."

"Are you sure?"

"He dead, Brody. Shot in da gut and broke his face on dem rocks."

"He sure looked dead."

Ames turned away from the edge. "Yer foot hurt?" He took Brody's boot in his hands and inspected it.

"No," Brody answered. "It just had a hold of my boot and pants. I bet I'll have a bruise though." He pulled his boot back on and tore a loose flap of his pants off. "Do you think he killed Joe?"

Ames waited a moment before nodding. "He done just dat, Brody. I'm afraid he did."

Looking away, Brody clenched his teeth and felt a prickling in his eyes. He fought away the burning urge to take his anger out on something. If Joseph was gone, Todd was an orphan.

"Let's go look, just in case." Getting up, Brody tested his legs. His heel was sore but everything worked fine. He went over and retrieved his gun. After blowing the dirt out of the action, he stood still for a moment, staring at the ground. "I don't know how to tell Todd."

"Ye can't worry bout dat right now. Let's go take a look, get dem horses, and figure a way outta here."

"I can't believe all of this has happened," Brody said. "I feel like it's a big nightmare and that I just need to wake up."

"Well, if ye is dreamin', I wish ye would wake up, too, cause we is in dis bad dream together. Ye sure know how ta get yerself in a pack o' trouble."

Brody went and stood by Ames, letting him lean on his shoulder. They both limped down the steep hill. "Did you see those cuffs on his wrists?"

"He done escaped from somewheres. Wish dey would have used bigger chain on dat mad-man. Could have save us a whole lot o' dad burn trouble. Ye know, Brody, ye is a brave man."

"I'm not brave," Brody said.

"I seen ye take on a bear and ye stood up ta ol' Frank and now ye took off and cornered dat crazy feller."

"I think I was the one who was cornered."

"I gonna be brave someday." Ames grinned.

Brody snorted, "You already are. You're the one who sent that monster over the cliff. You stuck with me. The real Ames stayed with me the whole time. You were as brave and sane as I've ever seen you."

"Ye mean not crazy, don't ye?"

Brody didn't answer.

Ames crossed his eyes and stuck his tongue out of the corner of his mouth. "How's dat?"

Brody managed a smile. "You're still crazy. You know that, right?"

They returned to the spooky cabin, and Brody started to search for Joe.

"Ye can start lookin' for yer friend, but I'm gonna get dese hosses ready to go. I ain't wantin' to be here when it turns dark."

Brody nodded, and stepped inside the cabin. The dirt floor was strewn with pieces of bone and scraps. The air was thick and musty.

Odd things hung from the walls, a necklace, a pair of boots, two old hats, and a woman's handbag. Reaching for the guns leaning against the wall, Brody took Joseph's shotgun and opened the barrel. He pulled the empty hulls out. After tossing them on the floor, Brody went outside and tied the gun to one of the pack saddles.

At the back of the house, he saw an old wooden structure that came up about waist high. It was much too short to be useful as an outhouse or storage shed. Curious, Brody walked closer. The top was solid except for a square opening not much bigger than his fist. The hole was worn smooth around its edges, as if it had been rubbed down over time.

Brody knocked on the top. "Joe?"

He examined the lid and found that it was hinged. On the opposite side he located a large hasp and rusty lock.

"Ames, come look at this." Ames finished fastening some more furs on top of the other horse, and limped over. Brody pointed at the large box. "Joe could be in here."

Ames looked the box over and knocked on the lid just the way Brody had. "Dat look like it been locked fer a while." He left, went to the lean-to, and returned with a hammer.

With a few hard whacks, the hasp broke loose and the lock fell. They pushed the heavy lid up and shoved it over, revealing a skeleton in the corner, covered in spider webs and a tattered dress.

Brody and Ames stared in shocked silence.

"Lordy," Ames finally said, breathing heavily.

They eased closer and peaked inside the wooden box.

"A woman," Ames said.

A pile of debris in the middle covered the skeleton's legs. The cone shaped pile had decaying vegetation at the bottom. Toward the top of the pile, the vegetation became recognizable. It was old, brittle flowers. On the very top was a handful of fresh yellow bitterweed blooms.

Ames stepped over to the lid and stuck his hand through the square hole in the top. "He been puttin' flowers in der fer a long time."

"That's what he meant," Brody said quietly. "He kept saying 'she is mine' and 'you never take her'."

"Never take her?"

Brody pointed to the skeleton. "I think he was talking about her."

Ames leaned in. "Dey's somethin' down here." He reached for a square shape sticking out from under the pile of decaying flowers. "A cigar box." He handed the dusty box to Brody.

Brody brushed the top off and opened it. It was filled with pieces of paper. As he looked through them, he found most were decorated with drawings. Under each drawing were a few sentences. He thumbed through the papers and read some of the words.

"He took me from the Fort Smith road in 1879. It has been three months since. He keeps a close watch but has brought me no harm. I fear that could change any moment."

"He knows not his own name. I have chosen to call him Joab. His mind is simple and he loves for me to draw. He thinks these words tell a story about the drawings. I pray someone will find me soon."

Flipping to another sheet, Brody found the sketch of a rabbit. He read some more.

"Though Joab woos me tenderly with flowers, trinkets, and odd things he finds in the woods, I still fear my life will end by his doing. Despite my hopes, no lawmen have come to my rescue in this hidden place."

The next page had a tree penciled in the middle with a squirrel on one of its limbs.

"I never knew any better hunter. This man is very possessive of me, and this spot he has claimed. I tried sneaking out a few days ago but he quickly found me."

Brody skipped a few sheets and read another.

"Joab speaks very little but protects me as if I were a child. Though I am here against my will, I feel safe with him. He brought me a gold chain today. I cannot imagine where he found it."

The next page had a very small drawing of a bird. Underneath it were several sections of writing.

"Winter has passed but I have lost track of the months. Joab has taken excellent care of me, and I am not sure I even want to leave anymore."

"He brought me the most beautiful flowers today and I cried."

"I am sick with fever and Joab tends to me constantly, but my fever has not broken."

"Two men stumbled upon our camp today. To my horror, Joab killed them with no warning. After taking their possessions, he offered them to me as gifts. I am too weak and saddened to write any longer."

Brody folded the pages and placed them back inside. "That's the last one."

"Her name in der anywhere?" Ames asked.

"I didn't see it."

Reaching out, Ames took the cigar box. "We gonna put it back."

"Shouldn't we take it and tell somebody?"

"We don't know her name or who ta tell. Dis her grave, Brody. Let's fix it all back da way it were."

They placed the box where they had found it and put the lid on top.

"He killed every person he came across and took their stuff," Brody said.

Ames brushed his hand off. "Didn't want nobody takin' his girl."

"It's not fair," Brody said. "Joe wasn't looking for trouble. He wasn't trying to take his girl. I mean, she's been dead for a long time."

"Not in dis feller's mind," Ames said.

They looked around the cabin for a while longer. Though Brody was desperate to find Joseph, he finally gave up. "I expected to find graves," he said to Ames.

"I ain't found nothin' else," Ames said.

"Where did he put those men he killed? Where's Joe?"

"Might never know," Ames said.

They found a way out the backside of the hollow and brought as much of the stolen items as the horses could carry. The trip was void of words while Brody thought about everything that had just happened. When they reached Joseph's camp, they stopped for the night.

It gave Brody an odd feeling to be staying at the site without Todd or Joseph. The woods were quieter than normal, not even an owl or whippoorwill made a sound.

At bedtime, Ames went over to the shed.

"I can't sleep in there," Brody said.

Ames looked inside the shack. "Me neither. It a small spot. Think I'll stay by the fire with ye." Ames closed the door and came over to join him. He placed his bedroll on the other side of the fire. "Get some good rest. We gonna leave early."

Brody put more wood on the flames and curled up in his blanket. "Thank you, Ames. I'd be dead right now if it wasn't for you. That man wanted blood and was ready to do me in."

Brody waited for Ames to say something but he remained quiet. "I just wanted to tell you how much I appreciated you coming out here with me."

Ames started to snore.

Brody laughed.

The loud snore stopped in the middle. "What?" Ames threw his covers back. "What are it?"

Brody laughed harder.

"Somebody coming?" Ames asked. "Ye all right?"

Wheezing with laughter, Brody said, "I'm fine. Go back to sleep."

The next morning, a loud moan woke Brody. Sitting up, he rubbed his eyes and saw Ames by the smoking fire pit.

"My ol' leg ain't working today," Ames said.

"It isn't broke, is it?"

"Naw. But it ain't wantin' ta bend. Got all stiff on me." He pulled his pant's leg up.

Brody got up and went over. "You've got a big bruise."

Holding onto Brody, Ames stood up but couldn't put much weight on his leg.

"Just lean against this tree," Brody suggested. "I'll get us packed up."

Ames propped against the tree and waited.

Brody paused. "Should we finish fixing Joe's wagon wheel and hitch the horses to it?"

Shaking his head, Ames winced. "I ain't got it in me."

"We'll leave it," Brody said. "I can get it later. Let's get out of here."

After rolling up the bedding and tying it to the horse's backs, he gathered the cooking utensils and food. When he had everything put in its place, he helped Ames onto the mule's back.

"You going to be all right?"

"In a day or so," Ames said. "I be good as new."

"I'll be right back," Brody said. "I've got to get Todd's things."

Brody went behind the camp and found the spot where he had buried his wooden crate. He uncovered it and pulled the box out of the ground. Peaking inside, he saw that all of Todd's things were still there.

Brody had wanted to see the smile on Todd's face when he brought his father home. That wasn't going to happen, and it felt shameful returning with nothing but a wooden box.

He went back to Joseph's horse and tied the box to a saddlebag. He ran a rope from the three horses halters, tying them in tandem. He handed Ames the lead, and he wrapped the rope around his saddle horn. Brody patted Buck and climbed into the saddle. He took one last look at camp, and then they left.

Before they reached the river at Fort Smith, Brody stopped.

"What are you doing?" Ames asked.

"Isn't this the trail that takes you back to Crawford County?"

Looking north, Ames cleared his throat but didn't say anything.

"You helped me track that monster in the woods, and you helped me find my parents. I'm going to miss you, but I know you have to get back and help with the planting."

Ames shifted in the saddle and wouldn't meet his eyes.

Realization dawned on Brody. "You're thinking about going with me, aren't you?"

Ames turned toward him. "Don't feel right, lettin' ye go talkin' ta dat lawman."

"You can't go with me. Your family needs you. You've got crops to plant."

"Dis mule is what dey need. I ain't gonna be much help. But it don't feel right. We been in all dis together, me and you."

"I'll be fine," Brody said. "Papa will go with me to see the marshal. I'll tell them about the killer and see if they will at least look for Joe's body."

"Dey might lock ya up."

"I can't keep running, and I've got to stop the Millers from messing with my folks."

"How you goin' do dat? Billy done got too powerful."

As bad as Brody hated to admit it, Ames was right. There was a big chance the Millers would never go to jail for their crimes, and an even bigger chance Brody could be sent in their place.

"Come stay with us," Ames said, "all of ya."

It was Brody's turn to look away. "We'll be all right."

"I reckon I'm just afraid I won't be seein' ye again."

Brody smiled. "I'll be coming to see you as soon as I can."

Ames handed him the lead for the three horses and then offered his hand. Brody shook with him. "I'll see you soon."

"Ye better," Ames said. "Ye dragged me off, chasin' a monster and got my leg all banged up." He laughed as he turned his mule north. "Ye gonna hafta come help with the fields."

Brody chuckled. "That wasn't part of the deal."

"I be seeing ye in a week," Ames said over his shoulder.

Chapter Eighteen

After Ames was gone, Brody sat and thought for a long time. If he went through town, a boy with three packhorses would draw attention, especially with all the furs and supplies on their backs. He would have to circle town again. It would take longer, but it was the only way to go unnoticed.

Keeping his head low and hat pulled down, Brody started the trip, hoping not to draw any attention. The man running the ferry tried to make conversation, but Brody pretended to nap while they crossed.

He left the river and started around town on a dim road. Warm winds swirled, blowing dogwood blooms across his path. The tumbling petals got caught in a tangled hedge of honeysuckle on the side of the road. He could almost taste the sweetness in the air.

He passed a white house and saw an elderly couple in the yard picking up dead limbs. The woman waved and Brody nodded to acknowledge her. At the next house, he noticed a pony tied to a wooden fence.

Brody pulled Buck to a stop. "Tater?"

The pony turned its head and looked at him. It nickered.

"It is you. What are you doing here?"

Looking farther down the fencerow, he could see two people setting a post in the ground. He recognized Daniel right away, but he had never seen the man that was with him. While Brody was weighing the risk of letting this man see him, Daniel spotted him.

"Mister Brody!" Daniel's wide smile stretched across his face, and his bare feet disappeared in the grass with each bouncing step. "Whatcha doin' over here?"

Glancing back, Brody looked to see if the elderly couple was watching. They were still busy with the yard work. "Hi, Daniel. I'm headed to see my folks."

"Where you get dem horses?"

"They belong to a friend of mine."

"Sarah say she needs to talk," Daniel said.

"To me?"

"Yes, sir. Made me promise to come get her first thing if I seen you. She say it's real important."

Brody felt a little flutter in his gut. "Did she say what for?

Daniel shook his head and patted Buck. "I real proud of you."

"For what?" Brody noticed the slender black man with Daniel was watching them. "Daniel, I don't want anyone to see us talking."

"Oh, he all right. Dat's my pa, Noah. He building a fence for some folks. He ain't gonna tell nobody." Daniel waved his father over.

The man came closer and reached up to shake hands with Brody. Noah added his other hand to the greeting and squeezed. "You're him, aren't you?" He smiled.

Brody tried to keep his face hidden with his hat. "Uhmm... I'm not sure —"

"You gave Daniel his pony."

"Yes sir."

Noah let go of Brody's hand and rubbed Daniels curly hair. "He's been takin' good care of him. We sure do appreciate it."

"I was glad to do it. Daniel's a friend of mine," Brody said.

Daniel stood straighter and poked his father in the arm. "Told you we was friends."

"Is it true that you're takin' the Millers down?" Noah asked.

"Taking the Millers down? I'm just trying to stay alive, although they'd be happy if I was dead."

"They has been talk about you putting them in their place."

"Oh, no sir. I'm not looking for a fight. Daniel just helped me get some stuff to the judge, and I was hoping that would be the end of it."

"The end of it? Them Millers ain't gonna stop, but they's a lot of people on your side," Noah said. "Billy and Frank been bad to a whole bunch of folks."

A wagon came around the corner and stopped at the first house in the curve. "I can't stay. I don't want people seeing me," Brody said.

"I'll get Sarah." Daniel pointed down the lane. "Dis here is Jenny Lind Road. Go on down till you hit Mill Creek, and we meet you there." Daniel untied Tater, climbed up, and rode toward town.

"Be home before dark," Noah called after him. Patting Buck's neck, Noah stared at Brody for a moment. "Take care of yourself."

"I will."

"I'd appreciate it if you'd watch after my boy too. He's my youngest and makes me laugh the most."

Brody slapped the reins gently and Buck headed down the road. "I'll do my best."

After reaching Mill Creek, Brody rode into the woods and waited. He tied Buck to a tree and skipped rocks across the water until he heard someone coming.

Tater trotted down the trail with Daniel and Sarah on his back. Sarah's dark hair waved in the breeze. Brody was about to smile and greet her when he noticed a scowl across her face. She seemed to be wearing one almost every time he saw her lately.

"Why would you do such a thing?" She jumped down from Tater's back.

Brody stepped toward her. "Do what?"

She walked right up to him, shaking her head. "Don't act stupid with me. You gave Eli a black eye."

"A black eye? I didn't hit him."

Daniel got down and leaned against a wide, old oak tree.

"You punched him at the river because you were jealous," Sarah said. "Didn't you?"

"I didn't do anything to Eli." Brody looked to Daniel and back to Sarah. "The Millers came and I shot Billy in the foot. I didn't punch Eli."

Daniel bounced over. "You shot Billy?"

"You shot Billy?" Sarah asked at the same time.

Brody tilted his head. "Eli didn't tell you? I didn't want to kill him, so I shot him in the foot."

Placing her hands on her hips, Sarah glared at him. "He told me you socked him in the eye."

"I'm telling you the truth. I didn't hurt Eli."

Daniel tugged on Brody's sleeve. "You shot Billy? I knowed you was gonna be famous."

"But I didn't...."

Sarah turned away. She started back to Tater.

"Don't come calling on me anymore," she said over her shoulder.

Brody's heart broke. "I don't understand what's going on."

"It is very simple," a voice said from behind him.

Eli slipped around the tree Daniel had been leaning against. He pointed his rifle at Brody's chest. "She does not want to see you anymore."

Sarah swung around. "Eli! What are you doing?"

"He's wanted," Eli said. Varying hues of purple and yellow marked the skin around his right eye.

"I didn't do that to you," Brody said. "Tell them the truth."

Eli waved the gun barrel. "Shut your mouth."

Daniel went to Tater's side. "I gonna get my pa."

Eli pointed the rifle at the boy. "You're not going anywhere. Get over here."

"Eli!" Sarah yelled. "Have you lost your mind?"

Eli motioned toward Brody and Daniel. "Sit down."

Daniel sat and pulled Brody down next to him.

Sarah stomped toward Eli. "What are you doing?"

He pointed at the ground. "You sit down too."

"You've gone mad!"

Eli took a threatening step toward her. "Sit down, girl."

She rolled her eyes, but plopped down next to Daniel. "Do you care to explain?" she said to Eli.

Eli stared at each one of them in turn. They stared back. He huffed. "I need to think."

"You *need* to put that gun away," Brody said pointedly.

Eli started to pace, keeping his gun pointed in their direction.

"Did the Millers give you that black eye, when we were at the river?" Brody asked.

Daniel leaned forward. "You tryin' to get reward money on Brody?"

"I didn't hit him," Brody said to Sarah.

"I'm believing you now," Sarah answered, glaring at Eli.

"Eli, you a big ol' liar," Daniel said.

Eli's face turned red. "Shut up! Shut up. Stop it."

Sarah stood up and pointed a stern finger at him. "That's enough. We're leaving."

Eli pointed the rifle at Brody. "No."

Sarah froze. "Eli," she said softly, "tell us why you're doing this."

He looked at her, and for the first time, Eli's expression softened. "I wish you liked me, the way you do him."

"Why don't you kill me then?" Brody suggested. "I bet she would really like you then."

Eli looked at him.

"Are you going to kill Daniel too?" Brody asked.

Daniel nudged Brody in the side with his elbow.

Brody didn't let up. "You're going to be a killer just like Billy and Frank."

It was quiet for a moment before Eli let out a long sigh. Lowering the rifle barrel, he looked from Brody to Daniel and then Sarah. "I'm not a killer. Billy..."

Brody pushed his hat up. "What happened? Did the Millers threaten you?"

Eli closed his eyes for a moment, then opened them. "Why couldn't you be bad? Why'd you have to be so nice?"

Brody was taken aback. He shot a confused look at Sarah.

Eli sat down on the ground, facing them. His shoulders slouched as he put the gun down in front of him. "I'm a Miller."

Daniel's voice squeaked. "A Miller?"

Brody stood and pulled Daniel to his feet.

"You said your last name was Johansson," Sarah said.

Eli nodded in shame. "I know. I lied. Billy is my uncle."

Sarah covered her mouth with her hand. "Why, Eli?"

Brody walked over to him. "That's how they found me down by the river, isn't it?" While he spoke, Brody pushed Eli's gun to the side with his foot.

Eli watched it slide away. "You don't have to worry. I'm not going to hurt anyone."

"You tried to get me killed," Brody said. "You led me right into a trap."

"I didn't know they were planning to shoot you. That's why I took cover when the blasting started."

Daniel stomped forward. "Big ol' liar. He knowed it fer sure."

"I didn't," Eli argued. "They tried to talk me into another ambush but I wouldn't."

Brody stared at him for a few moments. He didn't want to believe him, but there was something completely different about Eli now. He wasn't boastful or proud. He seemed truly embarrassed.

"Is that how you got that shiner? When you told them you wouldn't help with another trap?" Brody asked.

Eli nodded.

Sarah backed away from him. "You lied to me. You lied to me about everything."

Eli wouldn't look at her. "Not everything. My uncle told me to cozy up to you, to make you tell me where Brody was hiding. But it wasn't an act. I really do like you, Sarah. I'm sorry."

Sarah had pure venom in her voice. "So you just pretended to be interested in me because you were *ordered* to by your uncle?"

Eli sighed again. "My uncle told me which house was yours, and I waited for you to come out. I didn't figure on you being so pretty and nice."

Daniel leaned over to Brody, "Dat boy better stop talking. She gonna bury him deep."

Eli pointed at his eye. "Billy said he would give me a matching set if I didn't tell you Brody did it."

"I can't believe this," Sarah said. "I can't believe it."

"I'm sorry, Sarah. My Uncle Billy is-"

"I don't want to talk to you. Ever." Sarah stalked away.

"Why you follow us here?" Daniel asked. "If you ain't wantin' no trouble, why you come here and pull dat gun on us?"

"That's a good question," Brody said. "Why?"

Eli waited until Sarah was too far away to hear. "Because of her."

"What are you saying?"

"I saw Daniel riding that pony full out. When she jumped on and they took off, I knew they were coming to see you. I didn't want to shoot you. I was hoping to scare you off." He glanced at Sarah, standing by the creek. "I wanted you to go away, from her, for good."

Brody picked up Eli's gun and unloaded it. "I hate to disappoint you but I'm not going away. I'm going to the law with everything I know. The Millers will be in a fix."

Sarah came back over. "Let's go, Daniel."

Daniel looked to Brody and then to Sarah. "Where we goin?"

Her gaze stuck on Eli for a second. "Away from here."

Daniel brought Tater over and climbed up. "Where you going?" he asked Brody.

Brody put Eli's bullets in his pocket and leaned the gun against a tree. "I'm going around the south end of town, until I get home."

"Stay out of the prairie," Eli said. "Billy and Frank are out there, somewhere."

"Brody, that's right where you're headed," Sarah said.

Brody looked at Eli. "What are they doing out there?"

"I don't know." Eli spread his hands out, palms up "I really don't. Billy told me he was meeting Frank out there and for me to stay behind and watch his house."

"When?" Brody asked.

"Just a while ago."

"Why aren't you watching Billy's house then?" Brody asked. He saw Eli glance at Sarah. "Never mind. I know why."

Sarah gasped. "I saw Frank at the general store today, buying a lot of kerosene."

Eli jumped to his feet. His eyes grew wide. "Billy asked me what I did with the matches. Said he was going to have a bonfire tonight."

Grabbing Daniel's arm, Sarah pulled herself up on Tater's back. "We've got to warn your folks, Brody."

Chapter Nineteen

B rody ran to Buck, grabbed the saddle horn and swung up. "Y'all go back to town."

"No, sir," Daniel said, as he rode past.

"Sarah," Eli called.

Sarah yelled back, "Stay away from us. You've done enough!"

Kicking Buck in the sides, Brody sent him dashing down the road. The packhorses bumped into each other, trying to keep up. Within seconds, Brody had caught Sarah and Daniel.

"This is dangerous," Brody said over the pounding of the horse's hooves. "Y'all need to go back to town."

Daniel looked over and then hunkered down over Tater's mane.

"I'm sorry, Brody," Sarah blurted. "I let Eli fool me. Then I tried to use his friendship with me to make you jealous." She wiped at her eyes. "This is my fault."

"They would have just found another way to get at me." The road curved and Brody fought with the reins to keep Buck from pushing Tater off the path. "Daniel, take her back to town."

"No sir, mister sir. We goin'."

"We're going with you," Sarah said.

Brody gave up on trying to convince them otherwise. He wasn't sure what was about to happen. If the Millers were there, it wouldn't be good. He imagined seeing his folk's new place on fire. It would be a terrible loss, one he didn't think his mother could handle.

Brody expected to see smoke before they reached the house, but when the horses thundered into the yard, there was no one and no smoke to be seen.

"Maybe they're gone," Sarah said, sliding down.

Daniel reached over and grabbed Buck's reins. The horses breathed heavily and Buck snorted and pawed the ground. "Go check on 'em. I gonna hide your horses."

Brody dismounted and ran up onto the porch. Reaching for the door, his hand missed the handle as his father opened it.

"I thought I heard something," Papa said. He hugged Brody hard.

He leaned back into the house. "Polly, he's back. I told you Brody would come back."

"Brody," Momma said, her voice rising with excitement. Her footsteps quickened.

"Hold on," Brody said, stopping her before the hugging started. "The Millers..."

"They're coming!" Sarah yelled. "I see them."

Papa jerked Brody in the house but Brody tried to pull away. "My gun is with the horses."

Pushing him to the back of the main room, Papa opened the big wooden box used to hold the firewood. "You don't need a gun. Get in here." Wincing with pain, he pulled sticks of wood out and dropped them next to the box. "Get in."

"But I –"

"Get in," Papa ordered.

Brody climbed in and Papa closed the box. The firewood thumped against the lid, as it was stacked on top. The space was a little cramped but Brody was able to squirm around until he could peek through a knothole in the front panel.

He could only see Papa's legs as he went to get something from the side of the room and then walked outside. Momma's dress swished across the room and to the door. Horse hooves stomped the ground outside. The door was open, but Brody couldn't see past his mother and her dress.

"I told you not to come back here," Papa said.

"How's your ribs?" Brody recognized the voice as Frank's.

"Billy, you need to take your son and your men and get out of here," Papa warned.

Billy laughed. "I see you have your posse here with you." His voice was gruff. "I've got two bounty hunters here, lookin' for Brody Martin and Amos."

"Sarah," Momma said, "you and Daniel get on home. It's almost dark."

"Y'all stay right here," Billy said. "Get up there on the porch where we can keep an eye on you."

Brody heard footsteps on the porch and Momma stepped out of the doorway, allowing him a clear view of Billy, Frank, and two strangers in the yard. They were all still on their horses.

Billy had a shotgun across the saddle. Frank was holding some sticks with rags wrapped around their ends. One of the bounty hunters was wearing a brick-red shirt. He had a scraggly, black beard and a crooked nose. The other stranger was clean-shaven and looked younger, maybe in his twenties.

Papa shifted and stepped into Brody's view for a moment. He was holding a gun. "I've had enough of you."

Billy raised the shotgun barrel slowly. "I've got both hammers cocked. You know what will happen if you start shooting? I'm lettin' loose with both barrels." He gestured to the side, where Brody thought Momma, Sarah, and Daniel were standing.

"Y'all get in the house," Papa said.

"Stay put!" Billy nodded to Frank.

Frank struck a long match and held it under the kerosene soaked rags. The flames danced and Papa shifted his gun.

"Put the gun down," Billy ordered.

Papa hesitated.

Billy put the shotgun's stock against his shoulder and aimed at the porch. "Put it down or start shooting."

Frank reared back, as if to throw the flaming sticks on the roof.

Everything grew quiet while Papa waited. Finally, he lowered his gun. Frank got down carefully, holding the sticks in one hand. His horse shook it's head and sidestepped.

"Tell us where they are," the red-shirted bounty hunter demanded.

Frank jerked Papa's rifle away and handed it to Billy.

"They aren't here," Papa said.

"Everybody inside," Billy said. "Now."

"You will not come in my house," Momma said.

Frank stepped onto the porch. He pulled a pistol and pointed it in Momma's direction. "If you don't go inside, these torches will." He held the fire out, letting the flames lick the top of the doorframe.

Momma gasped.

Billy looked back to the bounty hunters. "Keep a watch out here."

After moving away, Frank tossed the torches into the dirt. Momma came through the doorway. She had one arm around Sarah and the other around Daniel. Sarah looked mad, but Daniel's eyes were as wide as they could be. He walked stiffly, as if afraid to turn his head.

Papa came inside and Billy limped behind him, keeping the double barrel ready. "Sit down. Everybody sit down."

Daniel sat immediately. Sarah and Momma were next and Papa last.

"Where's he at?" Billy asked.

"He's not here," Momma answered.

"I'm not talking to you. Where's he at?"

Sarah looked up. "I don't know."

Brody saw Papa glance at the wood box.

Billy leaned down and glared at Sarah and Daniel. His bushy mustache kept his top lip hidden. "Where's he at?"

"I don't know." Sarah stared at him and stuck her bottom jaw out.

A noise came from the front bedroom and Billy stood straight. "Go look," he said to Frank.

Frank opened the door and went inside.

"No," Momma said.

"So, he is here," Billy said.

"No, it's not him."

Brody heard Todd yelling. Frank came back into the room, dragging Todd by the arm.

Momma was on her feet in a second. "Leave him alone. He's sick."

Todd tried to bite Frank's hand. Frank shoved him to the floor, and Momma gathered him into her arms and sat back down. "Leave us be."

"Where did you find this little redskin?" Frank asked.

"A friend of the family," Papa said.

"I know Brody is here," Billy said. He pointed to Sarah and Daniel. "You two wouldn't be here if he wasn't."

"He's not here," Sarah said. "Why don't you leave him alone?"

"Leave him alone?" Billy asked, walking around the room. "Leave *him* alone? He killed my brother, stole my horses, took off with my sharecroppers, and gave my personal papers to the courts. I think it's *him* that needs to leave *me* alone."

"Then he shot you in the foot," Frank said.

Billy punched the wall and glared at Frank. "That boy is trying to put nails in my coffin! Nobody gets the best of Billy Miller. Nobody."

"We want some answers." Frank came closer and stopped in front of Momma and Todd. Momma hugged Todd tightly.

"Who is that?" Todd asked.

Brody looked toward Todd and was shocked to see him staring at the wood box.

Momma hadn't noticed where Todd was looking. "That's a bad man," she said while watching Frank. "A very bad man."

"Oh, I'm fixing to get real bad."

Todd's gaze stayed on the box for a moment. "Why is he in there?"

Brody cringed and eased away from the knothole.

Momma realized Todd had spotted Brody's hiding spot. "Frank Miller's in here because he's scared." She pulled Todd back so he couldn't see the wood box.

Frank pointed his pistol and shook it. "Woman, you better watch your mouth." Papa slapped the table, hard. Frank jerked around, red in the face.

"Frank," Billy said. "Check that other door."

Stomping across the floor, Frank disappeared into the other room. After a few moments, he came back. "Nobody in there."

Billy limped to the doorway and looked outside. "Brody! I know you're out there. Somebody's going to get hurt if you don't get up here." Billy came back over, took a water pitcher from the counter, and smashed it on the floor.

Daniel sniffed and a tear ran down his face. Sarah rubbed his hand.

"Billy!" one of the bounty hunters yelled. "Someone's coming!"

The sound of galloping horse hooves grew louder.

"Uncle Billy," Eli called from the yard.

Frank went to the porch. "What are you doing here?"

"I saw him," Eli said.

Sarah's jaw tightened and she squeezed Daniel's hand. Daniel wiped his face. Brody held his breath as a cold sweat came over his skin. Pushing against the end of the box with his feet, he shifted a tiny bit as quietly as he could, trying to get a better view while he waited for Eli's next words.

"I saw him in town," Eli said. "Just now. Hurry."

Frank went outside and Billy stopped in the doorway. "Are you sure it was him?"

"Yes, sir," Eli answered.

"Frank," Billy said, "shoot them mules around there. I don't want anybody following us."

Momma covered her mouth. "Not the mules, Jim."

Billy pointed the shotgun into the house. "Everybody stay put."

Shots rang out. Momma closed her eyes and pulled Todd's head under her chin.

"What about this pony?" Frank shouted.

Daniel jumped to his feet and ran out the door. Billy grabbed for him but was too slow. Billy raised the gun and stepped out of Brody's sight.

The shotgun thundered and Frank's pistol fired.

Papa and Momma rushed toward the door, but Papa stopped and held Momma back. "Keep the kids inside." He went out and closed the door behind him.

Brody shoved against the lid, knocking the firewood off the top. He heard his papa yelling and the sound of hoof beats on the ground.

Sarah yanked the lid off the box. Her face was wet. "I think they shot Tater."

Momma put Todd in the chair and told him to stay. She crossed the floor in a run and opened the door. Her hand flew to her face. "Oh, my Lord in heaven."

Heading to the door, Brody dragged Sarah along with him.

"Flint!" Todd yelled. He tried to come out, but Momma caught him and took him back inside.

Sarah clutched at Brody's arm as they came down off the porch. Tater was lying in the dirt, a streak of red running from the top of his head and down his neck. Papa was sitting next to him, holding Daniel. Daniel's arm was splayed out to the side. He was limp and had blood on his shirt.

Brody felt as though the weight of his whole body sank into the soles of his feet. He wanted to move but he was stuck in place. When he tore his boots free of the earth, Brody ran to his father's side.

Daniel was face up. His eyes were closed and his body was limp. His black skin had turned ashen.

Brody knelt next to them. Fear had nearly taken his breath. "Is he dead?"

"No," Papa said, "but he's hurt bad."

"Go get your father," Brody said to Sarah.

"They killed the mules, you'll have to go on foot."

Brody stood. "Daniel hid the horses. She can take Buck."

She looked to a small stand of trees across the pasture. "He took them in the woods over there." She sprinted away.

After a few minutes, she returned with Buck and the packhorses. She tied them to the porch and climbed onto Buck's saddle. "I'll be back as soon as I can." Sarah kicked the horse's sides and galloped away.

Tater started kicking and grunting, startling Brody and his father. His papa struggled to shield Daniel from the flailing hooves. "Help me get him out of the way, Brody!"

Brody lifted Daniel up and then held a hand down to his father. Papa groaned, but made it up, reaching again for Daniel.

The pony raised his head and struggled to get his feet underneath him. Tater had a pellet hole in his jaw and at the top edge of his head, just under the mane. His shoulder muscles shook.

"Tater," Daniel mumbled.

Papa said, "He's back on his feet."

Brody went back to Daniel's side. He took his hand. "I'm sorry, Daniel. This is my fault."

Papa shook his head. "Not now."

Brody nodded.

The door opened and Momma came running out.

"Where's Todd?" Papa asked.

"In the bedroom. What happened to Daniel?"

"He's got a buckshot pellet in his shoulder and another grazed his scalp."

Brody took a closer look at Daniel's head. He had a long gash above his ear.

Daniel moaned.

"Get him inside," Mama said.

Brody followed them into the house. Momma put an old quilt on the table and Papa laid Daniel on top. She pulled his shirt collar away from his neck and put a clean rag over the wound, trying to stop the bleeding. "Did the pellet go all the way through?"

Papa held out his arm where he had been holding Daniel. There was some blood on his sleeve. "It may have."

Daniel turned his head and looked at them. "Miller done went and shot me." He tried to touch his shoulder but Papa stopped him.

"You will be all right," Brody said. "Sarah went to get her father."

Todd came out of the bedroom. "Get back in there," Momma said.

He pouted. "I just wanted to see Flint and my pop." He turned back around and padded back into the bedroom.

Momma gave a sad frown. Both of his parents looked to Brody. He shook his head slowly. "I'll go talk to him."

"Maybe you should wait," Momma said. "Stay with Daniel and put gentle pressure on this rag. I'll go sit with Todd until the doctor gets here." She went into the bedroom.

Papa headed toward the front door. "Frank would not want to be seen with my gun, so he may have tossed it down the road. I'll be right back."

Brody nodded at him, then turned back. Daniel was staring intently at him.

"They gonna come back for you," Daniel said.

"You just close your eyes and be still," Brody answered.

"They gonna come back. Y'all should all leave."

"Nobody is leaving you, Daniel."

"Then they gonna kill you."

Chapter Twenty

Daniel rested while they waited on Sarah. Papa came back with his gun and lit the lanterns as the sun went down.

Mama opened the bedroom door. The soft glow of light fell on Todd. He was playing on the floor with Brody's old toys, a spinner top and a train his father had made out of a block of wood. She quietly shut the door behind her and went to check on Daniel.

Brody told a little about what he and Ames had found, skipping the parts where he almost died in the traps, and about the razor sharp claws... and when he almost fell off the cliff. It was a very short story.

When Sarah finally arrived, it was full dark. She opened the door and her father came in behind her.

"Doctor Slaughter," Papa said, greeting him.

"Mr. Martin. How is he?" Doc put his bag on the table.

"He got hit in the shoulder and side of the head."

"Bring a lantern closer and let me take a look."

Papa raised the lantern over the doctor's head. Sarah came to Brody and held his hand. Her palm was hot in his.

"Are you all right?" he asked softly.

"I can't believe all this happened. The Miller's will pay for this."

"Sarah." Her father cast a dark look her way. He saw the hand-holding and his frown deepened.

She let go of Brody's hand. "Daddy, today they shot Daniel and his horse, and they killed the Martin's mules. That's after threatening to burn their house down and pointing guns at all of us."

"Sarah Elizabeth, don't argue with me. You shouldn't have been over here."

She stormed outside.

Momma came out of the bedroom. "How does it look?"

Doctor Slaughter moved Daniel's arm around while feeling of his shoulder. Daniel whimpered. "It went clean through. I've got the bleeding stopped but he's going to need stitches above his ear. I'll give you a little Laudanum," he said to Daniel.

"He's going to be all right?" Brody asked.

Doctor Slaughter gave Daniel a sip of liquid from a dark bottle. "He will be all right after I stitch him up. He'll have to take it easy for a while and keep those stitches clean."

Sarah appeared back in the doorway. "How's he doing?"

"Fine." He pulled some thread from his bag. "Hold him still."

Papa patted Daniel on the arm and then held both of his hands tight.

Momma came closer. "Hold still, Daniel. It won't take long."

After threading the needle, Mr. Slaughter went to work. "Get in the buggy, Sarah. We can't be here long." He caught Papa's stare. "The Millers will be back. We'll be leaving soon."

"What about Daniel?"

"We'll take him home." He looked at Momma. "All of you should leave."

Momma cleared her throat. "I'm ready."

"Brody and I are going to the sheriff tomorrow," Papa said.

Doctor Slaughter huffed. "That's what Billy wants."

Daniel squirmed. "Ouch."

Papa adjusted his grip on Daniel's hands. "Why would Billy want us to go to the law?"

The doctor tied off the last stitch and snipped the thread. "The Millers have half the town in their pocket, even the lawmen."

"You're telling me we shouldn't report what the Millers did here tonight?"

"That's what I'm saying."

Papa let go of Daniel. "We have to go to the law. They can't keep doing things like this."

Stepping closer, Momma rubbed Papa's shoulder. "You should listen to him. We have Brody back, and we need to do what's best for him. We have to take him away from here."

"I'm standing right here," Brody said.

Papa gave him a stern look.

Looking from Papa to Momma, Brody said, "I don't want you moving because of me."

"We're staying together," Momma said, "and it's not safe here anymore."

"It's never been safe here," Papa argued.

Doctor Slaughter wrapped Daniel's shoulder with a bandage. "Mr. Martin, the Millers have been doing whatever they wanted for years. A few people have tried to change that, and they aren't around anymore. Several business owners tried taking a stand against Billy, and he paid their competitors to lower their prices. You can imagine what happened."

"He ran them out of business," Papa said.

"You won't win against the Millers. I'm a fool for even coming here tonight. I could be next on Billy's list." Mr. Slaughter picked up his bag and went to the doorway. He paused. "I've been needing to say something. I don't want your boy coming around Sarah anymore."

Brody's cheeks burned when he heard the doctor's words. He had deep feelings for Sarah and couldn't imagine never seeing her again.

"Daddy!" Sarah wailed from the porch.

"Hush, Sarah, this is for your own good."

Mr. Slaughter looked back before going outside. "When your son is around, she's in danger. Tonight proves that." He stepped down off the porch. "Bring Daniel to the buggy. We'll take him home."

Brody tried to think of something to say to Sarah's father, anything to change his mind, but he couldn't pin down the right words. Brody started outside, but Papa laid a hand on his arm and shook his head. "Give me a minute with Doc."

Momma hugged Brody. "I'm sorry about Sarah, but Doc just wants to keep her safe. We feel the same way about you, too."

Sarah appeared in the doorway. "Mr. Martin convinced Daddy to let me say goodbye."

Todd popped out of the bedroom. "Can I come out now?"

Momma looked from Brody to Sarah and then went over to swoop Todd up. "Let's go outside for a minute."

"Is Father out there?"

Mama hugged him close.

Brody swallowed hard. "I don't want you to go, but your father is right."

"Don't say that," Sarah said.

"You're not safe around me." Brody cleared his throat. "Nobody is. You should do what your father says."

Standing still, Sarah seemed to be thinking, maybe considering what to say.

"Time to go, Sarah," Mr. Slaughter called.

She rushed toward Brody. Her arms wrapped around him and she squeezed. Brody returned the hug, just as tightly. There was nothing awkward about the moment. It was wondrous and he wished it would never end but Sarah broke free from the embrace and ran out the door.

After slowly lowering his empty arms, he went to the doorway. Sarah had climbed into the buggy, and Daniel was propped against her. The doctor was taking a look at Tater.

After a few moments Mr. Slaughter turned to Papa. "One of the pellets creased him. It just knocked him out for a bit. A bit lower, and Daniel's little pony would be dead." He tied Tater to the back and got in.

Sarah turned around to face Brody. The tears in her eyes glistened in the light from the carriage lanterns. "Goodbye, Brody." Doctor Slaughter slapped the reins and the buggy jerked forward.

A long sigh escaped Brody as a weight settled on his shoulders. He had ruined so many lives. He should never have come back to Fort Smith.

Papa came over and laid a hand on his shoulder. "This has been a rough night." He turned to where Momma sat in the porch rocker.

"I want to go check if the mules are really dead." Momma nodded and handed him the lantern. He disappeared around the side of the house.

Todd dashed onto the porch and grabbed his hand. "Flint. I saw the treasure box. You brought it."

Brody forced a smile. "I sure did."

"We have to hide it." Todd yanked on his arm. "We have to hide it right now or the bad men will get it."

"I need to talk to Papa when he comes back," Brody said.

Todd began to cry. "Those bad men are going to get my treasures."

Momma got up from the rocker, her features hard as rock. She paused by Brody long enough to say, "Get your stuff together. We are leaving."

Brody tried to follow her inside, but Todd gripped his wrist and stopped him. "No, we have to hide it."

"What's the matter?" Momma stepped back into the doorway.

"It's his treasures."

"My father gave 'em to me," Todd said.

"We can take them with us."

"Noooo," Todd pleaded. "We need to bury them. Please?"

Papa came around the corner of the house. "What's on your mind, Polly?"

"We are leaving," she said, turning back inside.

"Leaving? Where to?" Papa shut the door behind him. In a moment, both of them were raising their voices.

Brody stepped down from the porch. "Let's get your treasures off the horse."

Todd smiled but his happiness disappeared quickly. "Did you find him?"

"Not yet," Brody said.

Todd remained silent for a moment. Instead of fidgeting around, he just stared at Brody. He seemed to be waiting for something. Brody imagined he wanted to hear some kind of magic words, something that would make his father appear in a puff of smoke. If only it were that simple.

"We can take the treasure box with us. We can play hully gully with your marbles."

"No," Todd said.

"No?"

"I don't want to see that stuff. Not yet. Not till Father comes back."

Nodding slowly, Brody leaned against a porch post. He saw the bone and turquoise necklace around the boy's neck. "You're wearing his necklace."

Todd pulled it over his head and held it out. "Can we save it in the box? Can we put it with my treasures? Please? Will you hide it for me, Flint?"

Brody could see his folks through the window. Momma stomped across the room, carrying clothes and food from the cupboard. Papa was right behind her. It looked as though he had lost the argument of staying in Fort Smith.

Brody knelt by Todd. "We can take the box with us."

"No," Todd said. "You said not to keep treasures in camp."

"There's a stretch of woods behind the house. We can hide it among the trees."

Todd put the necklace in his pocket and smiled. "We can hide it good, Flint, so no one can find it."

Brody started to stand but hesitated. "I need to tell you something."

"What is it?"

"Flint isn't…" Not sure how to tell him, Brody shifted uncomfortably. "My name is Brody."

"But you're Flint," Todd said.

"You and your father call me that, but my real name is Brody." He waited to see if Todd understood what he was saying.

"Like Father calling me his cub? Can I still call you Flint?" Todd asked.

Brody grinned. "You can call me whatever you want."

Papa opened the door. He had an armload of bedding, and he didn't look happy. "Your mother says we're leaving. We will camp at the back of the property tonight and leave at first light."

Momma came up behind him. "Jim, we need to hurry in case they come back."

She shoved a gunny sack toward Brody. "Carry this. It's food."

Brody took it to Buck and tied it to his saddle. Papa stacked things on top of the furs on the packhorses. "We need to unload that stuff," Brody said, "so you and Momma can ride."

"We may need some of this," Papa said. "You and I can walk. We're going just far enough to keep them from finding us tonight."

"You really think they are coming back?"

Coming to their side, Momma untied Buck's rein. "Do you have the lanterns?"

"Right here," Papa said.

"Brody, will you put Todd up on those furs?" Mama pointed at Todd. "Young man, I expect you to hang on tight and don't fall off."

Todd grinned and held his arms up. Brody heaved him onto the furs.

"This is Father's horse." Todd leaned forward and patted her. "Hi, girl."

Brody waited for Todd to ask where Joseph was again but he didn't.

Momma put a foot in one of Buck's stirrups and Papa lifted her up by the waist. She settled into the saddle and said, "Let's go."

Papa led the packhorses and Brody carried the chest with Todd's treasures. The spring frog-peepers were filling the air with their shrill calls. Momma kept fussing at Todd to be still and quit acting like a wild child. Before long, they had reached the trees.

"They won't think to look back here," Papa said. "If they come back tonight."

"They'll be back." Momma helped Todd down and started untying the bedding. "I know you didn't want to leave, but I couldn't have slept in the house."

Papa hung a lantern on a limb, and Brody helped him stretch and tie off a large sheet of canvas. "We'll leave early, as soon as the sun comes up," Papa said.

Todd piped up. "Where are we going tomorrow?"

No one answered.

"Where are we going?" Brody asked.

Momma sighed. "We're not sure."

"Father can't find us," Todd said. "He can't find us, Flint." His eyes began to fill with tears.

Brody held the wood crate out for Todd to see. "Let's go hide your treasures."

Todd took a deep breath and nodded. After lighting a second lantern, Brody and Todd walked away from camp. A rocky wash wound it's way among the roots. Brody found a strange looking tree to use as a marker, tried to guess which direction he was facing, and then counted his steps to a big oak. Todd followed along behind him.

Placing the box at the base of the oak, Brody scraped at the ground. It was hard and stony, so he began covering the small chest with rocks and limbs.

Todd pulled something from his pocket. "Wait. Put the necklace in there."

"Are you sure?"

Todd dropped it in his palm. "I'm saving it for when he comes back. Mawme gave it to him before she died."

Brody held back his sorrow for the little boy.

After putting the necklace inside the treasure box, Brody and Todd stacked branches and stones on top.

Todd's effort started strong but quickly faded until he picked up a rock and just held it. "Is my father ever coming back?"

Taking the last stone from Todd's hand, Brody placed it on the pile. "I... I'm not sure where he is."

Todd stood. "I think he will."

"Maybe he will, then," Brody said.

They scattered leaves across the secret spot and headed back toward camp. As he walked, Brody thought about Joseph. He knew he would never return, but Todd still held hope, a child's hope, false hope, and that troubled Brody's heart.

Chapter Twenty-One

After Papa built a tiny fire, he got Brody to help him drag dead limbs over. They stacked them on the side of the fire that faced the house. "Let's cover these branches with leaves. I don't think there is any way they can see this small fire from that far away, but I want to be sure."

When Papa was finished, he rested on a log next to the fire. Momma sat next to him. Brody plopped down on the opposite side with Todd.

Todd yawned. "Can we stay here?"

"Just for tonight," Papa said. "We are headed out tomorrow."

"But Father won't know where –"

"We'll talk about it in the morning." Papa's rough voice almost sounded like a snarl.

"Jim." Momma glared at him. She stood and took Todd's hand in hers. "It's time for bed. Come on."

Todd got up and went with her. Brody watched as Todd flopped onto the pile of furs and blankets. "Can Flint sleep by me tonight?" Todd asked.

"Of course," Momma said.

Brody's gaze went back to his father. Papa stared into the fire, rubbed his face hard, and then watched the flames again. Brody opened his mouth intending to break the silence, but Papa spoke first. "We shouldn't be running off."

Brody scooted closer. "What should I do?"

"Son, I don't have the answer anymore. I thought I had it all figured out, but what happened tonight changed everything."

Momma came back over and sat. "Tell us what really happened while you were gone." She lowered her voice. "I know you well enough to spot holes in your tale earlier. So you did not find his papa, not even a body?"

Brody shook his head. "No."

"What happened?" she asked. "Where did those horses, furs, and traps come from?"

He was confused as to why Momma would be asking about horses, after everything that had just happened. "This first. We have to figure this out first."

She looked from him to Papa and back again. "What?"

Gesturing to the fire and them sitting on the ground, Brody said, "This. What are we going to do?"

"We are leaving Fort Smith," Momma said. "It's decided."

"We can't just keep on running," Papa argued. "I don't feel like any sort of real man, letting those devils run me out of my own home."

Momma gave him a stern look. "You know we have to do what's best for our family."

Brody scowled. "I should never have come back."

"Brody Martin, it broke our hearts when we lost you. You're my only child, and can you fathom the horrors I imagined you were going through. We will figure this out, and we will keep our family whole."

Everyone sat in silence after the outburst.

"Well, then where are we going?" Brody finally asked.

Placing her hand on Papa's knee, Momma said, "We can go back to our old cabin."

"We can't go there," Papa said. "That's one of the first places Billy will look."

She moved her hand. "He's going to be looking in Fort Smith."

Papa looked to Brody. "When Billy doesn't find you in town, he will go there next."

"We can be gone by then," Momma offered.

Wrinkling his brow, Papa looked at her. "Gone?"

"We can stay there a few days and then move on," she said.

Papa's voice grew louder. "We can't go off blind like that."

"Do you have a better idea?" She shook her head. "No, you don't."

The muscle on the side of Papa's jaw bulged. "Give me some time to think."

Momma snapped back, "Jim, we don't have time."

Brody stood. "Stop it!"

The heated conversation between his parents grew quiet. The fire crackled and snapped. His mother stood and looked in the distance.

Momma's voice was mournful. "They're burning our home, Jim."

Papa stood and stared into the night. Brody turned and saw an orange glow on the horizon. It was too far to see flames, but the eerie flickers of light illuminated smoke rising into the air.

Clearing his throat, Papa looked at Momma and took her hand. "I'm sorry. You were right about them, Polly."

Momma put her arm around his waist. "At least we have what is most precious to us." She turned her head to look at Brody.

Brody walked into the darkness. He had caused all of this. His family had lost two homes because of him. Todd had lost his father because he wasn't there to help. Daniel and Ames had also paid a terrible price for being in his company, and then there was Sarah. Brody couldn't let anything happen to her.

He stopped walking and listened to an owl hooting in the distance. The lonely call brought back memories of the first night he spent alone in the foothills of the Devil's Backbone, blind and scared. It seemed like it had been a lifetime ago that he had struggled to survive on the mountain.

The soft glow of a lantern pushed the darkness back. "What are you doing?" Papa asked.

"Thinking."

"Me too."

Brody watched bugs bouncing off the globe on the light. The larger ones lived, but the tiny ones burned up and died. Memories of Joseph and the reward poster came back to him. Everything on the poster had disappeared when Joseph threw it into the fire. Brody wished with all his might that life could work the same way, and that you could just throw it into a fire and all the bad things would burn away.

"Let's go back to camp," Papa said. "I'll stay up. You need some rest."

Brody joined his father and they headed back. While walking next to him, Papa put his arm across Brody's shoulders. "I swear you have grown another foot. You've got a few more scars on you, too."

Brody felt comforted. "Those furs, supplies, and packhorses belong to Todd. Joe's shotgun is there too."

"It was an honorable thing you did, Brody, going back to look for his father. I'm proud of you. You've grown into a fine young man."

They returned to the dying fire and saw that Momma had lain down on the fur pallet next to Todd.

"Get some sleep," Papa said.

Brody nodded and lay down next to Momma. She reached over and rubbed his arm. "We will be fine," she said quietly.

After saying his prayers, he got real still and watched Papa, sitting by the fire. Brody knew there was only one thing he could do. There was only one way his family and friends would ever be safe.

Papa gently shook him. "There's just a few hours left before daybreak, son. Can you take the watch?"

Brody nodded, and his father finally lay down on the furs. Brody waited until he heard him snoring softly. Quietly, he went to his saddlebag, got his pencil and left a short note by the fire.

After placing a stone on the paper to hold it down, he stood and watched the waning firelight dance across the three figures on the pallet of furs. They were his family, even little Todd. His heart was heavy.

They loved him unconditionally. They loved him so much they were willing to leave everything behind, just to keep him from being hurt. Joseph had been willing to die too, leading that monster away from his son. That was a powerful kind of love.

Now, he needed to do what was right to protect those he loved. He needed to show that same powerful kind of love. Sighing, he quietly went to Buck's side.

He seemed to be making a habit of sneaking away from his folks. The thought sent a pain through his heart. He wanted to stay but couldn't. His actions and decisions were causing pure torture to his Momma.

It has to be this way. Brody untied Buck and led him away from camp.

Having left the camp unguarded and his father asleep, Brody decided to make sure the Millers where nowhere around. He used the light of the half moon and headed toward the farm. It was still dark as he approached the property with caution. He stopped, watched, and waited. The eastern sky started to glow with the rising sun, and when he was convinced there was no trap, he rode up to the smoking timbers that use to be the farmhouse. A smoldering beam fell, and he pulled back on Buck's reins.

The crisp dawn air was refreshing, and Brody heard the faint crow of a rooster in the distance. It promised to be a fair morning, except for the two dead mules in the pen, a burnt house, and the spot of blood in the yard from where Daniel had been shot.

"Brody."

Brody unslung the Henry and snatched it to his shoulder.

"Wait," Eli said, as he stepped away from the little barn and into the open. His hands were raised, and there was no sign of his rifle. "It's me."

Fearing a trap, Brody brought his gun to bear on him. "Who's with you?'

Eli raised his hands. "No one, I swear it." He slowly lowered his hands. "I saw him shoot Daniel. How bad was it?"

"Doctor Slaughter said he's going to be all right." He glanced around, still nervous about finding Eli at the farm. "Why are you here?"

"I heard they burnt the house. I had to come and see if…" He glanced toward the rubble. "I thought they might have killed everyone."

"We left. My family is long gone."

"I need to warn you," Eli said.

"About what?"

"They won't give up. Billy is so mad. They didn't even come home this morning. I guess they are still looking. He's going to keep coming for you."

Brody slowly lowered the rifle. A rage came up inside of him, but he kept his voice flat. "Let him come back. Everyone is gone. I'm headed for Indian Territory."

He knew the Millers wouldn't stop. They would keep after his family and friends, threatening them for information about his whereabouts. "Go tell Billy what I said. Tell him I'm alone and headed across the border. He can come and find me whenever he's ready, but he needs to leave my folks and friends alone. They don't know where I'm headed. I didn't even tell them I was leaving."

Eli nodded. "I'm sorry, Brody. I didn't know it would get this messed up. I'm not like them. I promise."

Brody studied Eli's face. He wanted to believe him.

Reaching to his side, Eli pulled a long knife out of his belt and held it out. "Here, it's yours."

Brody rode closer. The sight of his lost knife warmed him inside, tamping his anger back. "Are you giving it to me?"

"It wasn't right for me to keep it." Eli put it in Brody's hand.

After giving it a quick inspection, he put the knife in his pack and the gun back in the leather sling. He climbed down and stared at Eli for a moment. Brody's right hand clinched into a tight fist. With all his might, he punched Eli right in the nose.

He fell like a tree, hit the ground, and then scrambled backwards. Holding his bloody nose, he got back to his feet. His legs were a bit wobbly. "I guess I deserved that."

Brody rubbed his smarting knuckles. "Consider it even?"

"We're even," Eli said.

"Thanks for giving me my knife back." Brody got back on the horse. "And I really appreciate the help last night."

"It was the right thing to do." Eli fished in his pocket and pulled out a handkerchief. He wadded it under his nose. "I'm not good enough for Sarah, and I know it. She really likes you, and that was worse than a bee under my hat when I was trying to get her to like me." He chuckled ruefully. "Now I think she would shoot me as soon as look at me."

Brody felt a little sorry for hitting Eli, even though it sure had made him feel better.

"When Uncle Billy had your family at gunpoint last night, sending them off on a rabbit trail was the only thing I could think to do. They were pretty chapped when they couldn't find you, but they figured you had beat your horse through town and headed for the hills."

"Thanks for that. You may have saved people I love from being killed." He reached down and Eli shook his hand.

Turning Buck to the side, Brody looked down the road. "I have to get going before my folks come looking for me. Make sure you tell Billy I'll be waiting for him in Indian Territory. I don't want him thinking I'm with my folks."

"I'm sorry I tricked you," Eli said.

"Me too." He nudged Buck with his heels and headed down the road.

Keeping the horse at a trot, Brody made his way around Fort Smith as fast as he could, keeping off the main roads in case Frank or Billy were still looking. As soon as he got on the ferry, he started talking to the men taking him across.

"Do you know the Millers?"

A short fellow with bulging muscles laughed. "Everyone knows them."

Brody pulled his hat up and scratched his head, purposely exposing the scar on his face. "Billy or Frank will be coming this way. Make sure you tell them I crossed here."

The men looked at him, curious. One of them asked, "Is Billy a friend of yours?"

"Oh, we know each other well," Brody said.

The ferry reached the bank. Pulling his hat back down, Brody rode off the long raft and headed for Indian Territory. His trap was set, and when the Millers came looking, he would lead them on a wild goose chase they would never forget.

After a couple of miles, he turned Buck to the left and entered the woods. He reached in his pack and found his knife. Feeling the familiar handle in his hand gave him some comfort. It was good to have the family heirloom again.

He started thinking about his parents, afraid to rebuild their house because some bad men could burn it down around them again.

Why?

He pulled Buck to a stop.

Why?

Why had his life taken this path? The harshness of the world had closed in on him and wrapped its cold hands around his heart. Everything he cared about had been utterly ruined.

He took a deep breath and belted out an angry yell to the sky. "WHY?"

Buck jolted at the sudden outburst. Brody jumped down and picked up an old rotten limb. The section was three feet long and parts of it crumbled as he lifted it above his head. He brought it down hard, throwing and smashing it against the base of a tree.

"Why?" He clenched his jaw and squeezed his hands into tight fists. After a moment, he relaxed and turned toward the horse. "I don't understand, Buck. I lost my family and my friends. I don't have a home. We don't have a home."

He wrapped his hands around Buck's neck and hugged him. "We don't have a home." Buck nickered and lipped at his shirt.

Brody let go and picked up a piece of punky wood that had broken off the rotten limb. He squeezed it and watched it crumble into hundreds of pieces. He didn't belong anywhere, and no one was safe around him. Turning his hand over, he let the last bits of wood fall to the ground.

After brushing his hands off, he turned his palms up and looked at the tiny scars and callouses that crisscrossed his skin. He dropped them to his side. "I don't know what to do now."

His choices were countless, however, all of them seemed wrong. The best option in Brody's mind was to crawl under a rock and disappear forever, but he couldn't. He would wait for the Millers to come and make them regret it.

The high-pitched cry of a child came from nearby. Listening closely, he thought he could make out faint voices too.

Brody left Buck behind and went closer to the trail. He moved fast, but as quietly as he could. Using the trees to hide behind, he worked his way forward until he was within eyesight of the road. Just as he crouched down in a gulley near the track, two rattling buckboard wagons came into view.

Through the gaps between the trees, he could see both of them clearly as they passed. The beds were filled with grown-ups. Couples of varying ages were holding each other closely. There looked to be twelve men and twelve women, and some of the women were holding babies.

One of the men banged on the back of the wagon's seat. "I'm telling you, we paid for our land! Miller said it was ours, free and clear."

The Millers. Their crookedness reached all the way into Indian Territory.

"Quiet down," the driver said. "We'll let the judge figure this out."

Several men on horseback rode close to the wagons. They were carrying rifles across their thighs.

"They are bringing in squatters," Brody whispered.

The man that had banged on the seat turned back to the woman next to him, and Brody got a good look at his face. He had a set of twin scars on his cheek and a milky eye.

The sound of children talking grew louder. Behind the wagons, were lines of barefoot, ragged, tow-headed kids. Two little girls at the front were holding hands and sniffling. They were not more than six years old, and both were dirty and wearing patchwork clothes. Behind them, the line of kids continued. Boys and girls kept walking by and Brody began to wonder how many there could be.

Their faces were streaked with tear tracks that had collected dust from the trail. Never had he seen a poorer group of people in his life. They had nothing except the tattered clothes on their backs.

At least twenty kids had gone by, before Brody started to count the rest of them as they passed. Slipping closer to the road, he started a tally in his head. The line kept coming and Brody's number kept growing. When he reached one hundred, he could hardly believe it.

Their bare feet shuffled along and the number still grew higher. As the last child went by, Brody's count reached one hundred and twenty. He guessed at least twenty had passed before he started keeping track, so the total was around one hundred and forty kids.

During his amazement of how many there were, Brody failed to stay out of sight. The last child in line noticed him. The boy looked to be Todd's age, around seven or eight. He had stopped walking and was staring at Brody. His eyes were swollen from crying.

The child wiped at his face. "We don't have no place to live no more." Turning, the boy rushed to catch up with the others. The road curved into the woods, and Brody lost sight of them.

He sat cross-legged, and pondered what he had just witnessed.

There were so many children, and each of their lives had been turned upside down. Most of those kids would probably be taken to an orphanage or picked up by farmers needing cheap labor. Their folks would more than likely end up in jail. The Millers had done this to them.

Brody didn't blink for a long time. Billy Miller was a worse monster than the crazy man Ames threw over the cliff. His son was a coward and just as cruel, and they kept getting away with it. It made him furious.

Brody went back to his horse, grabbed his reins and swung up. "Life could be worse, Buck. I've just seen it."

Raising his fist in the air, he shook it hard. "Come and get me, Billy. I'm waiting!" He rode out to the trail. As he turned toward Joseph's camp, he glanced over his shoulder. Two figures caught his attention. Brody stopped Buck and looked back. In the curve of the road were two riders. One was wearing a brick-red shirt, and they were watching the line of kids go by. The bounty hunters!

Chapter Twenty-Two

B rody kicked Buck hard and headed deep into the trees. He kept checking over his shoulder but saw no sign of the men. There was no time to prepare for the Millers and their henchmen.

Buck's legs became a blur. Brody rode him longer and harder than he knew he should have. Thinking he had gained ground on his pursuers, Brody slowed Buck and turned farther into the woods, cutting across country toward the camp.

Racing through camp, Brody headed to the west line and stopped long enough to gather some traps. He tossed them down and inspected their condition. They were starting to rust. Normally he would boil and wax them, but this time he only needed to catch one more thing… a man.

He knew the coyote traps wouldn't hurt anyone, but they would slow them down, and just like the crazy trapper's trick, it would alert him that someone was coming. He needed the traps to stop them for a moment, just long enough for him to set his plan into action.

Brody set three traps around the shed. The leaves worked well to hide them. When he was finished, he started a fire in the pit and went to the edge of the woods. From his position, he could see the dim camp road, the fire, and the shed. Miller's men would think he was near the fire or in the shed. They would go to the shed and step in one of the traps. He imagined firing a shot in the air, circling around, and then leading them on a long trek through the woods. He would set traps as he went, making it a trip the bounty hunters would never forget.

The night trudged onward and his eyelids grew heavy, but the bounty hunters did not come. Even though he had lost them, Brody knew it was only a matter of time before they found the camp. At daylight, Brody curled up on the ground behind a massive oak and slept.

Two nerve-wracking days passed, but the Millers and the bounty hunters never showed. He set more traps and refined his plan, deciding he would lead them to the spooky gorge with the hanging traps with metal teeth.

The saddlebag had no more food inside and neither did his stomach. "Buck." Brody gave a low whistle and the horse ambled over. "Let's go hunting."

After putting his rifle in the scabbard, he climbed into the saddle and nudged Buck's sides with his boots. The horse plodded along while Brody thought. He was having second thoughts about his plans. He wanted to lead the Millers and their men into the middle of nowhere, wearing them to a frazzle. They would step in traps, get caught in briars, covered in ticks, trip, stumble, and suffer.

He thought about how the mad-trapper had fallen over the cliff. Brody wanted the same thing to happen to the Millers. He wanted to hurt them, to make them pay for everything they had done. Those feelings scared him. He didn't want to be that kind of person, yet these men were bad, and they continued to ruin people's lives.

He took Buck around a cedar patch and up a gentle slope. When they reached the top of the hill, he pulled back on the reins and stopped the horse. The hollow below was filled with mature oak and hickory trees. While watching for any movement in the woods, he lost track of time. He began to wonder why the bounty hunters had not shown up yet. What if they had gone to find Ames instead?

Something black moved between some trees below. Shifting in the saddle, Brody pulled the Henry out. He placed the homemade stock against his shoulder and waited. A turkey came around a tree, stopped, and looked back. After a moment, more turkeys followed. They pecked at the ground and leaves. Their heads bobbed and jerked as they looked for danger.

Brody wanted to climb down for the shot, but his movement would send them running. He guessed the distance to be a hundred steps. It would be a very difficult shot. He brought his hand away from the trigger and up to the rear sight, moving very slowly. After adjusting the sight, he returned his finger to the trigger.

Picking out the biggest turkey, he aimed. Brody paused and imagined facing the Millers. Could he shoot a man if he had to? His heart began to race.

He fired and the turkeys scattered. Some ran, some flew, and his almost-supper was with them. They flapped their wings wildly, battering the air, but their heavy bodies kept them from flying far. Remaining motionless, Brody waited.

One of the smaller hens banked in his direction and started a glide toward the ground. Just as the turkey landed, Brody jacked another round into the chamber and aimed.

The hen snapped her head around. *Chirp. Chirp.*

Brody shot and the turkey went down, its wings flailing for a moment. Instead of going over to collect his meal, he sat and stared at the bird. In the background, he could hear the other turkeys running through the woods.

He put the gun away and patted Buck's neck. "You barely spooked. I swear you are the best horse ever."

After getting back to camp, Brody went to the shed and got a pan. He put the turkey on a stump and spread the feathers on its breast, exposing the skin. Poking his knife tip through the skin, he cut a slit down the front and pulled the skin away from the meat and legs. When he was finished, he cut both sides of the breast meat from the bone, picked a few stray feathers off, and tossed the breast in the pan. Pushing the legs back, he made another cut and located the ball joints in the hips. Cutting the tissue and meat around the joints, released the legs. After chopping the feet off, he added the drumsticks to the rest of the meat.

Before cooking the turkey, he cut the breast into thinner strips and stoked the fire. When the flames died down and left glowing red coals, he placed the pan in the middle.

While he waited on the meat to cook, his thoughts went back to Ames and the Millers. He wondered if Joseph's camp was too secluded. What if the bounty hunters had given up? Or what if the Millers had headed north to look for Ames while their men searched Indian Territory? Either way, Ames could be in danger. Brody thought of how he had managed to find him. It did take a while and he had to ask around, but he had found their farm in one day.

He couldn't keep waiting. The situation with the Millers had grown much worse and he had a feeling, a bad feeling. If the bounty hunters couldn't find him, they would look for Ames next.

Buck nickered and snorted. The horse's ears were forward as it watched something behind Brody. Holding his breath, he resisted the urge to turn around. He listened and watched Buck stare. The Henry was still on the horse and too far away to reach quickly. The hunting knife was closer. He had left it on the other side of the fire pit, on top of the stump.

Brody sprang forward, jumped over the pit, and ran toward his knife. Without a pause, he grabbed the weapon and slid to the ground behind the stump. He expected to hear shots or shouted orders from the Millers, but nothing happened.

Slower than a snail, he rose up. An old Indian was standing right where Brody had been kneeling by the fire. He was clothed in brown leather, and his leggings were fringed with beads. Hanging in front of the leggings was a breechcloth. The rectangle piece of deerskin had a design across the bottom. White and black feathers were attached to the collar of his vest. The man's deep brown skin was wrinkled and creased. He held an ancient bow at his side. The wood was old and dark with age, but the string and arrow looked new.

"I'm not a trespasser." Brody stood up slowly. "I'm not a squatter."

The Indian lowered his head, which was shaved except for a single, wispy lock of long gray hair coming from the very top. His sharp gaze went to the knife in Brody's hand. Bringing the bow up, he pulled the arrow back and aimed.

"Wait!" Brody dropped the knife and threw his hands out in front of him.

The old Indian's face remained stern, and a stressful moment passed. Finally, the man's nostrils widened as he sniffed. The smell of burning meat was filling the air. He nodded, ever so slightly, toward the pan in the pit.

Brody looked to the smoking meat and back to the Indian. "It's a turkey I shot."

The meat sizzled and the smoke thickened. Pointing with the arrow tip, the man gestured toward the pan again.

"You want some?" Brody reached over with his foot and pushed it off the coals and toward the man.

The Indian's expression never changed but he took a step back, lowered the bow, and slowly released the tension on the string. With no warning, he let out a shrill *whoop*.

"Wait," Brody said. "I was trapping with Joseph and Todd. I'm supposed to be here."

Another *whoop* came from the woods east of camp, and Brody knew he was surrounded. Staring at the Indian, he waited and worried over what they would do to him.

The man's attention turned to the other side of the camp-shed and Brody saw a large figure emerge from the brush. Brody tried to move but was rooted to the spot. "Joe!"

Joseph looked much different. The side of his face was swollen. His neck had a large, half-healed cut that ran up to his ear. Another fresh wound was on his forearm.

Brody's throat tried to close from all the emotion welling up. He choked out, "I thought you were dead."

Looking at him with pleading eyes, Joseph held out his hand. There were four empty Henry rim fire cartridges in his palm.

"Where is Todd, Brody? Where is my son?"

"He's alive, Joe. Todd's with my folks."

Joseph closed his eyes for a second and took a deep breath. "Take me there."

"I'm not sure where my family has taken him. They are running from the Millers. Billy has sent bounty hunters after me, so I'm not safe to be around."

Joseph said something to the old Indian in a language Brody didn't understand. The Indian spoke back, emphasizing some of his words with his hands.

Joseph looked at the cartridges in his palm, and then threw them down, scattering them in all directions. "These men will not stop us from finding my son."

∾ The End ∾

Devil's Trap facts...

▫ Native Americans who chose to adopt civilized life often took Christian/English names. The 1885-1940 Cherokee census list Indian names in one column and their English/Christian names in a second column. *See the Indian Agency Census Rolls at Accessgenealogy.com*

▫ Trapping was an important part of life in the 1800's. Territory was fiercely protected. Pelts were traded, sold, and stolen.

▫The Devil's Backbone is a long ridge located south of Fort Smith, near Greenwood, Arkansas. The Union and Confederates fought a battle on the ridge, in the edges of Indian Territory, on September 1st, 1863. General Cabell was defeated by the Union forces at the base of the ridge. A majority of his men retreated without orders and abandoned the battle.

▫Hully Gully is a real game originally called, "Ana foni" (bones) by the Choctaw. Their version of the game wasn't played with marbles. They would recover a certain platelet type bone found in the joints of game animals like deer. It is circular in shape and they would dry it in the sun and conceal a number of them in their hands while playing Ana foni which later became known as Hully Gully to us.

▫The Estes General Store was a business in Fort Smith. Research shows ads in 1881 placed by Estes General Store in Fort Smith newspapers stating they were looking for furs to purchase. Trapping declined in the late 1800's mostly due to the railroad bringing in cheaper materials from overseas.

▫The Boston Store opened on Garrison Avenue in 1879 and remained in business until 1984.

▫ The creature Joseph refers to as Tsul 'Kalu was a Cherokee legend. It meant slant eyed or sloping giant and is believed by some to be the Cherokee version of Bigfoot.

▫Mr. Birnie was a real undertaker in Fort Smith during this period.

▫Wampus Cat, also called Whistling Wampus, is a Cherokee legend with many versions. It resulted from the curse of a Native American medicine man. While the name Wampus Cat is not as well known today, it's actually widespread. Schools that use the Wampus Cat as a mascot include, Conway High, Arkansas – Clark Fork High, Idaho – Atoka High, Oklahoma – Itasca High, Texas – Leesville High, Louisiana – and Charlotte Amateur Football, North Carolina. *See one version of the legend at AmericanFolklore.net. or search YouTube "Wampus Cat by D. Tabler."*

▫The Marshal Reeves that Joseph mentions is a real historical figure. He was possibly the first black U.S. Marshal (1875). Bass Reeves served as marshal for 32 years. The famous Belle Starr surrendered to him. Bass also arrested his own son, Benjamin, for murder. Marshal Reeves was born a slave in Crawford County in 1838. During the Civil War, Reeves fled into Indian Territory and lived with the Cherokee. During his career he was shot at many times but never wounded. He killed 14 outlaws in the line of duty and arrested 3,000. *See a bronze statue of him at Pendergraft Park in Fort Smith. Fort Smith Museum*

▫Billy The Kid and Jesse James were famous outlaws during this period. Billy(William Bonney) had evaded the law for years but was finally cornered by sheriff Pat Garrett in December, 1880. Billy was captured and put in jail. He was sentenced to hang but killed two guards and escaped. Again, Pat Garrett tracked him down. Billy was shot by Pat and died in July 1881. Jesse James was also near the end of his career of crime. Jesse fled to Missouri and was killed in April 1882 by a fellow outlaw.

□Chinese, Irish, and German immigrants started filtering into the Arkansas Delta in the 1840's. Some came to escape wars in their countries. Others were lured by promises of cheap farms and higher wages. In 1881, a Chinese person was still a rare sight in Arkansas. A 1900 census only shows 62 Chinese residents living in the state.

□Hoffman Grocery opened in 1878. *"It is a first class grocery store in the little frame structure on the avenue lately put up by Mr. Picci near Joe Sherman's wagon shop." Fort Smith Weekly New Era. July 24th, 1878.*

□The September hangings of the Manley brothers, that Daniel mentioned, occurred on September 9th, 1881. The Manley brothers killed a farmer in the Creek Nation on Dec. 3, 1880, and attempted to murder the farmer's wife and children. William Barnett was a hired hand on the farm, and survived the attack. He was wounded and lost his left hand during the ordeal. Barnett testified against the men and they were hanged with three other criminals in Sept. 1881. *Fort Smith Museum*

□ In May of 1881, the *Arkansas Traveler Newspaper* stated there were 109 prisoners in the tiny jail located in Fort Smith. The conditions were horrid. The men were cramped and many had become sick.

□The Wildman of Indian Territory was based on a real event in history. While it's unknown when the man started killing, his first verified victim was in 1883. *Read the amazing, true story of "The Panther" and about some of his 16 victims at JamesBabb.wordpress.com, or TheOsageTerror.blogspot.com where you will find links to newspapers articles from the 1800's.*

James Babb

▫ Doctor Slaughter was a real doctor in Fort Smith.

▫ Squatters and trespassers were a big problem in Indian Territory. The scene Brody witnessed really happened and was described by stories in the *Muskogee Journal* and the *Arkansas City Traveler* in 1881. '*Lieut. Shoemaker and Gov. Jack McCurtain, of the Choctaw Nation, are hard at work removing intruders, and such a set. The effects of a dozen families could all be placed in one wagon with room to spare, but the 12 men and 12 women have 144 red-headed, tow headed, shock-headed urchins of all sizes, tagging along after them barefooted, and more also. There being no provisions visible, it is a wonder how they lived. They have remained there because forbidden to do so if ordered by the United States to remain, they would have skipped out in one night. It's no wonder Arkansas papers howl over the enforced exodus from the Indian country if that State is to be afflicted with such a class of shiftless emigrants.*'

Todd's Treasure Box – Is It Real?

Everyone loves a good treasure hunt. Was Todd's treasure really hidden? Make sure you read The Devil's Den(2015). Do Brody and Todd go back for the wooden box? Or, is it still hidden and waiting for someone to find it? Find out in the last book in the series, The Devil's Den.

James Babb

Acknowledgments

I'd like to thank my friends and family for all of their help.

My readers have kept me writing and I appreciate every one of you. I am continually amazed at the number of Brody's fans. I hope you enjoy his adventures.

The Fort Smith Museum and Library were a tremendous help with the research.

A special thanks goes to Mike Bailey for teaching me all about trapping, and to Brenda Dickerson and Leslie Mansur for all their help & support.

About the Author

To find out more about award winning author James Babb
and his ponderings, you will want to check out his blog at:

JamesBabb.wordpress.com

Or for the facebookers of the world:

Facebook.com/TheDevilsBackbone

Facebook.com/james.babb.376

James Babb

Coleman's Story as written by
Joanna Pearson

Coleman Daniel Pearson was 13 when a mosquito infected him with Eastern Equine Encephalitis(EEE). He went to Heaven on October 22, 2013. Coleman had a loving heart and demonstrated it in his actions and words. He always told everyone "I love you" when he was leaving or getting off the phone. He protected anyone being bullied and on one occasion, gave his shoes to someone being harassed for not having name brand shoes. He made everyone feel important and special, building up the confidence of others and accepting them regardless of their age, race, religion, or lack thereof. He enjoyed hunting, fishing, and football, so he frequently roamed through the woods with older brother Caleb in pursuit of whatever happened to be in season, or played football in the yard with his younger brother Clay.

Most of all, Coleman loved Jesus with all his heart and demonstrated his faith daily through his speech and actions. Coleman wanted to make people's lives better, he even told us that if anything happened to him we should donate his organs to save others. Being infected with EEE made his wish impossible, but we knew he would want us to do everything in our power to prevent anyone else from enduring the ravages of EEE, thus the Coleman Daniel Pearson Foundation began to spread awareness of the mosquito-borne Eastern EEE and Arbovirus. On October 22, 2013, Coleman became the first case the CDC has confirmed in Arkansas. It cycles between mosquitoes and birds in freshwater swampy areas (making Arkansas the perfect habitat). The virus is capable of infecting mammals, birds, amphibians and reptiles and causes severe illness in humans and horses.

Coleman was seen by his pediatrician on September 30, 2013 for headache, muscle pain, tiredness, and a slight fever, and was given an antibiotic. He did not tell the doctor, but later mentioned having tremors in his hands. He had been bitten by mosquitos on September 27th between Ben Lomond, Arkansas and Little River on a camping trip. He went to school all week, played football on October 3rd, went to the high school game on the 4th, then spent the weekend with friends riding 4-wheelers and having fun. On October 6th he complained of headache and fever and was going to get some Ibuprofen when he began having seizures. He was ultimately airlifted to Arkansas Children's Hospital where his condition deteriorated from talking and moving, to being intubated, put on a ventilator in an induced coma, to his death from multiple massive strokes on October 22, 2013 all from a mosquito bite…..

Symptoms normally develop 3-10 days after the bite of an infected mosquito and begin with a sudden onset of fever, drowsiness, tiredness, muscle pains, and a headache of increasing severity. Symptoms can become more severe over 1-2 weeks and infected individuals will either recover or show onset of encephalitis characterized by seizures, vomiting, neck stiffness and focal neurological deficits (speech, hearing, or vision problems). People under the age of 15 or over 50 seem to be at greatest risk for severe disease. It is one of the most serious mosquito-borne diseases in the United States. There is currently no vaccine for humans, although the government has an active trial study going through the military. Typically in the United States six cases per year are confirmed in humans, with Florida reporting the highest rates of one or two human cases every year. Florida averages over 60 cases of EEE in horses each year and can exceed 200. Arkansas needs a system for reporting horse deaths, as we learned after Coleman's battle, that numerous horse deaths had occurred in the area around the time he was bitten. Horse deaths are a good warning for people to take extra precautions.

Precautions: Keep areas of stagnant water drained. Make sure window screens are intact if you have windows open. Avoid the outdoors, especially wooded areas, at dusk & dawn. Wear clothes that cover as much skin as possible, then use mosquito repellant with DEET, and carry a Thermocell. If you are bitten by a mosquito tell your family and watch for symptoms. In Arkansas we now have West Nile, St. Louis Encephalitis and Eastern Equine Encephalitis that are all contracted from a mosquito bite and are all in the Arbovirus family.

Enjoy the lakes, rivers, and forests of Arkansas just like Coleman always did, but be aware that a mosquito can be more than a nuisance, it's bite can be more deadly than a water-moccasin or rattlesnake…

Please visit these sites for more information on EEE
http://www.cdc.gov/easternequineencephalitis/
http://en.wikipedia.org/wiki/Eastern_equine_encephalitis_virus

A letter to Coleman: by Ethan Erwin

All the fish that swim the rivers, and the ducks that fly the sky
Could never replace the feeling of losing you big guy.

It hurt so bad that you left us, and the tears they fell like rain.
Even thoughts of the good times couldn't ease the pain.

But when we think of all the people gone to meet God in the sky,
they say, "when they get where they're going, down here we shouldn't cry."

Cause you're up there with your papaw Pete, and Jesus and all his friends.
And you don't have to feel the pain you felt down here again.

I smile when I think about it, I don't wonder if you're there.
Cause you help God paint the sunsets, and they're the most
beautiful sights to bear.

Mom and dad they miss you a bunch, I'd say everybody does.
Caleb, Clay, and Cody and I. You're the heart and soul of us.

But we'll take care of your brothers. The rest of your Blue Tick Gang.
So you go on to Heaven and in our hearts, remain.

Made in the USA
Charleston, SC
30 June 2016